"They probably know we're here," Pete continued. "There're only three saloons in town. I saw them in the one three doors from the hotel."

Laredo pointed to the rear door. "Let's hook up and get outa here. We can be gone an hour before they find out."

"You haven't had anything to eat."

"I'll eat later."

They led the sorrel out of the stall and hooked up. Pete went to open the rear doors of the stable as Laredo climbed onto the wagon seat.

As the doors opened, there was a fusillade of shots.

Also by Arthur Moore
Published by Fawcett Books:

THE KID FROM RINCON

TRAIL OF THE GATLINGS

Arthur Moore

FAWCETT GOLD MEDAL • NEW YORK

A Fawcett Gold Medal Book
Published by Ballantine Books
Copyright © 1989 by Arthur Moore

All rights reserved under International and Pan-American Copyright Conventions. Published in the United States by Ballantine Books, a division of Random House, Inc., New York, and simultaneously in Canada by Random House of Canada Limited, Toronto.

Library of Congress Catalog Card Number: 88-92214

ISBN 0-449-13426-1

Manufactured in the United States of America

First Edition: February 1989

11 10 9 8 7 6 5 4 3 2

Chapter One

A HALF hour after midnight four men came clattering up to the main gate of the Pendleton Stage and Delivery Lines. They drove a light spring wagon with a two-horse team and all wore the regulation Pendleton overalls of warehouse workers, dark brown with the distinctive PSD over the left breast.

The driver wrapped the reins around his thick wrist and pulled out papers, presenting them to the blue-clad guard.

"Howdy, neighbor, nice cool night . . ."

"Yep." The guard, a beefy, round-shouldered man, peered curiously at the four. He had never seen any of them before, but of course Pendleton was a large company and he'd never worked at the other warehouse. He grunted and took the papers inside to the light. They had come to get machinery parts: six crates.

The second guard in the shack asked, "What is it?"

"They pickin' up some crates."

"Late as hell f'that, ain't it?"

"Yeh." The guard shuffled the papers; they seemed to be in order. Of course the shift manager in the warehouse would be the judge, putting his signature on the proper line. That part of it was no skin off his ass. The guard went back out to the wagon and handed the papers over. "What you doin' here so late?"

1

The driver, a rangy man with a black mustache, shrugged. "Thass the first thing we ast, too. They said go git the goddam boxes. So here we are."

The guard nodded. That was the way it was. He signaled Jess and the roadway barrier rose in the air.

The team shoved into the collars and the wagon rolled through, the other three men stared at him as they passed. The guard went back into the shack. "Funny they sent four of 'em to handle some crates. I thought they was allus yelling shorthanded over to the town warehouse."

"Yeah, funny," Jess said.

The wagon was out of sight of the guard shack in moments; it was a large yard, the main terminal of the Pendleton company. It had a railroad spur and was on the main road for east and west stage and freight travel. The yard was just outside the city, about ten miles from the river.

The wagon veered left, following the railroad tracks that shone dully in the dark night. The main warehouse was to the right, well-lighted, where crews worked round the clock. There were other, smaller buildings, all of them locked at this hour.

Three boxcars loomed up, dark and silent in a forest of shadows. Clete Anderson said, "It's the last car." He snapped his fingers. "Who's got the lantern?"

He halted the team and Alvy Bowen struck a match and held the flame to the oily wick. It sputtered alight. "The numbers is on the side of the car." He handed the lantern to Fred Orne.

Fred lifted the lantern high and compared the numbers with a bit of paper. "This's it." He swung the light. "It's got a goddam big padlock."

Alvy moved close to the car's sliding doors. Carefully he positioned a steel pry bar and pulled down on it steadily. The dry wood gave with a splintering sound as he forced the hasp out. The padlock clattered onto the hard ground.

Clete said, "Easy with them doors . . ." He glanced toward the distant guard shack, then pushed as Alvy pulled and the heavy door moved, protesting every inch. The interior was black till Fred turned the lantern into it. "There they are."

There were six stacked crates. Stenciled on the unpainted wood were black letters under the bursting bomb emblem of the Ordnance Department: WOODRUFF ARSENAL US ARMY. Three of the crates were smaller, nearly square, labeled: AMMUNITION.

Fred stepped from the wagon onto the freight car and put the lantern on the floor. "Let's get to it . . ."

It took a half hour to transfer the six heavy crates to the wagon; it was necessary to work as silently as possible in the feeble light.

Even so, they were overheard.

As Ira and Clete stretched the tarpaulin over the crates, one of the guards appeared. He came on them suddenly in the gloom. "What the hell youall doin' here? You supposed to be at the goddam warehouse!"

Alvy said, "No, we ain't. Look at this here." He held up the square of white paper. Fred lifted the lantern and as the guard stepped close and reached for the paper, Ira Page hit him at the nape of the neck with the pry bar. They all heard the bone snap.

Ira caught the body and eased it to the ground.

"Goddammit," Clete growled. "All right. Let's shove 'im in the car."

"There wasn't nothing else we could do," Ira complained. "He come snoopin' around."

"Lift 'im into the goddam car."

They rolled the body in and pulled the sliding door closed. Clete motioned them and blew out the lantern as they climbed into the wagon. Alvy grabbed the reins and turned the horses.

They rode back to the main gate and stopped at the barrier.

There was only one guard in the shack. He came out, frowning at the wagon. "Where's Jess?"

"Who's that?" Clete asked.

"The other guard."

Clete shook his head. "We ain't seen him."

The guard looked at each of them and at the tarpaulin-covered load. "Let's see your papers."

Clete protested. "You looked at 'em when we come in."

"Lissen, you know the rules. I gotta see you had the papers signed off."

"Yeh, all right," Clete said wearily. He got down and fished in his pocket, following the guard into the shack. He gave the other the folded papers and as the man turned and held them under the light, Clete drew his revolver and hit the guard very hard on top of the head, catching him as he fell.

He laid the man on the floor, took the papers and climbed back into the wagon. Ira had already released the barrier and they drove through and turned left onto the road leading south.

They drove steadily for more than an hour and watched for a turnoff, a wooden fence, marking the side road. In a short time they approached the river. It was colder here with a light mist hiding the far shore.

The river road was rutted and bumpy; the heavy crates shifted and slammed into the sides of the wagon. There were a few boats moored here and there, mostly fishing craft or flatboats with a few poor souls aboard.

It took another half hour to reach the barge that they'd tied up the day before. It was a black hulk in the night, low in the water, with a large cabin.

They halted and transferred the crates and covered them again with the canvas. Clete said, "Humbolt's fifty miles down the river. We'll tie up at Grannie's place and meet you there."

"Yeh, good." Fred Orne nodded and went back to the

wagon. He would return it to the livery where they'd rented it and ride south in the morning.

They were all being paid off at Humbolt. It had been a nice, easy job.

Chapter Two

THE badly hurt guard in the shack was found within the hour as the third man of the guard crew returned from his regular rounds. He sounded the alarm immediately and the warehouse manager sent men for the doctor and the city police.

The disappearance of the other guard, Jess Baskin, remained a mystery until the middle of the afternoon when someone noticed that the padlock was missing from the freight car. When the door was pushed back the body was revealed—as well as the loss of six government crates. Federal authorities were notified at once and detectives were assigned to the case.

The federals were three men headed by Harold Kiskadden who decided, after a look around, that the robbery was an inside job. How had the robbers known the crates were there unless they had seen the documents? The murder was easily explained; the guard had happened upon the robbers.

He set about, with his men, interviewing all the employees of the company. That took the best part of a week and brought in no usable information. No one knew anything.

"Somebody's lying to us," Harold said grumpily.

He was forced to report to his superior: no progress. He did not say in the report that he had ignored the city police and made his own judgments.

Harold Kiskadden's superior was John R. Fleming, Chief of Security Operations—West. He worked out of the Treasury Department in Washington, D.C. Fleming did not have a high opinion of Kiskadden because of previous investigations, but he followed procedure in ordering him to Lockhart.

He was not at all surprised when Kiskadden fell over his own feet; Fleming had expected nothing better. And it left him free to order the Tanner Detective Organization—TDO—into the breach. Tanner worked almost exclusively for the government in one capacity or another.

Fleming sent a messenger for Hector Tanner, one of the two sons of the founder, Hugh Tanner. The sons had taken over the day-to-day operations of the firm; Hector was in charge of investigations.

Fleming was a large, paunchy individual who smoked cigars constantly; his office always had a layer of smoke and smelled stale, which Fleming seemed cheerfully unaware of. Hector Tanner entered, a skinny, gray man of forty winters, his quick eyes darting everywhere. He took his usual chair and waited, wrinkling his nose at the tobacco smells.

"A robbery," Fleming said heavily. "Some bastards got wind of a shipment of Gatlings, broke into a freight car, killed a guard and got away."

"Where?"

"A town called Lockhart, out in Oklahoma Territory."

"A rough part of the world."

"Yes, pretty wild."

"Gatlings . . . how many? How'd they happen to be there in the first place?"

Fleming made a face and puffed blue smoke. "Three, with ammunition. Enough fire power to wipe out a regiment of battalions." He passed over a folder. "They were on a siding awaiting shipment. The railroad would have moved them out in another day or so. Whoever took them knew the schedule.

It's all in there. Put some good men on it. Those guns in the wrong hands—'' Fleming raised his arms pantomiming an explosion.

Hector glanced through the folder. But he knew it would all be in order. Fleming, despite his terrible habits, was thorough. He got up. "I'll get men on it immediately."

"Good. Keep me informed."

"I will." Hector went out and took a long breath in the corridor. The worst thing about dealing with the government was Fleming's cigars.

Tanner headquarters was only a few blocks distant and Hector walked them quickly, thinking about Gatling guns. Where was the best market for them—Mexico? Probably. That country was in a state of turmoil. What if the guns were consigned by the thief to be sold there? Three Gatlings could be the difference between small-time guerrilla fighting and immense power. The guns could be worth a fortune to someone!

And they had already caused one death . . . and a man near death.

In the building he went at once to the office of Jim Bowers, manpower expert, and let him study the information folder.

"Who do we send? It needs a Westerner, I expect."

"Yes, someone from the Bluestar unit." Bowers scratched his chin. He moved to the large hand-colored map on the wall, studded with different color pins. "We've got a man not too far from the Oklahoma Territory now." He tapped a finger on the map.

"Who is it?"

"Laredo Garrett. Maybe you remember him from that railroad job a few months ago."

"Yes, I read the reports. But isn't he young?"

Bowers smiled. "Young and agile. Hell of a good mind and tough as nails. He comes from Kansas. You were in Interior once. D'you remember John Spence Garrett? He was young Garrett's father."

"I recall him vaguely. . . ."

"You know Hannibal Thatcher."

"Oh, yes. He was my boss at Interior."

"Well, Hannibal hired young Laredo as a guide for surveying crews on the plains. You ask Thatcher what he thinks of Laredo."

"All right. Laredo is in Bluestar?"

"Yes. He and Pete Torres were both put into it about two years after Barksdale, the Tanner training center."

Hector stared at the map, hands in his pockets. "Well, if you say so, but I'm surprised they're in Bluestar so young. That's an elite unit."

"It certainly is. Go back and read the report on that railroad job again. No one could have cleared it up better."

Hector smiled. "Very well. He seems well recommended, Jim. Get a wire out right away. Time is important."

"Let's team him with Torres—any objections?"

"None at all. They've worked together before?"

Bowers nodded. He went to the door. "I'll get the wire off now."

Laredo received the wire at his hotel in Dakota Springs. It was a dusty little burg of perhaps a thousand souls; the hotel had four rooms, none much better than a tent. He had just finished investigating a case of suspected murder, but had found the murderee alive and well. The man had planned his own "death" in hopes of escaping a pile of debts.

It was a long wire, much of it in the Tanner code, and he was delighted that Pete Torres would meet him in Lockhart. He got out a map and looked up the place. About three hundred miles away . . . by road and train.

Three Gatling guns stolen in a daring midnight raid! It looked to be a very interesting case. He packed a bag and went down the street to the stagecoach office and bought a ticket.

He was a well-setup young man with tawny blond hair and

regular, rather square features. There was a lithe quickness about him that a number of opponents had noticed in confrontations and wished they had worried about more, subsequently.

The stageline took him into Lockhart after a week's travel, arriving late at night. He took a room at the nearest hotel and slept for eleven hours, waking ravenously hungry.

In the morning he rented a small buggy and drove to the Pendleton yards, giving his name at the main gate. He was expected. He was taken to see the manager, Tim Laiksen. Laredo presented his credentials and Laiksen ushered him into a cluttered office and offered him tobacco and a chair. Laiksen was a big, red-haired man who looked as if he had come up through the ranks and could probably still work alongside any of his men at the hardest tasks.

"We had government detectives here," he said to Laredo, "and they wasn't worth hot spit. Never found a thing."

"I'm not strictly government. I work for Tanner. The government retains us. I understand one of your men was badly hurt and is in the hospital. May I speak to him?"

"That's Nyall Rozak. Yes, he's laid up. Don't know if he can talk yet. Somebody hit him on the back of the head. Tried to kill 'im I guess. He got a full head o' hair. That saved him, the doc said."

Laredo wrote down the address of the hospital. "I'd like to walk over the grounds, Mr. Laiksen. Will you have someone—"

"Do 'er myself. Glad to." The big man got up and they went out to the yard. Laiksen pointed to the main gate. "They come in there, about midnight. Had to have 'em a wagon. All ours is accounted for. They drove down there to the tracks where they was three boxcars settin'."

Laredo noted that the position of the boxcars was out of the line of sight of the main gate. He said, "So the thieves had to somehow know that the Gatlings were inside the car."

10

"That's right. That's what them detectives figgered too. But they never found anyone."

"They went right to the boxcar, tore off the lock, and hauled away the crates."

"Yep. That's the lock right there." It was hanging from the broken hasp.

There was a dark bloodstain inside the freight car where the body of the other guard had lain. Laiksen saw him looking at it. "That's where they put Jess Baskin. We think he musta got suspicious and come snoopin' down here and they killed him."

Laredo nodded. Very likely. He put his back to the boxcar and regarded the big red-haired man. "All right, Mr. Laiksen, tell me who knew the guns were inside this car."

Promptly, Laiksen said, "Four of us knew. Me, the yard boss, Hank Stella, and two clerks. I told all that to them other detectives."

"Yes, of course. But that question is the key to this whole business. Did you steal those guns, Mr. Laiksen?"

For a moment the big man's eyes grew hard—then he grinned. "You joshin' me, ain't you?"

"A little bit. Where can I talk to Mr. Stella?"

"I'll get him for you."

They crossed the yard and went into the big warehouse. To one side on the ground floor was a long shedlike room where a half dozen clerks in shirtsleeves worked at tables. In a cubicle off that room a thin, whipcord man stood at a waist-high table writing in a ledger. He turned as Laiksen called.

"This here's Mr. Garrett from the government, Hank. Wants to ast you some questions."

Laredo did not contradict the manager. He shook hands with Stella. "It's about the Gatling robbery, sir."

Stella nodded. He seemed wary, Laredo thought, then said, "I'm told you're one of four men who knew the guns were there."

11

"Had to know," Stella said in a tight voice. "Can't do this here job wi'out knowing what we got."

"I understand that. Who stole the guns, Mr. Stella?"

Stella's brows furrowed and his mouth became a hard line. Laiksen said, "He's joshin' you, Hank."

"Don't like smartass kids comin' in here with fool questions." His fists were doubled up. Stella had a short fuse, Laredo thought. Were his reactions those of a guilty man?

Laredo said, "It would be easy for you to recrate those guns and ship them to any point, wouldn't it?"

Stella swung at him. Laredo easily avoided the punch, slapped a second punch away and turned Stella, shoving him to the wall. "We're just talking, Mr. Stella."

"You sonofabitch! You accusin' me of—"

"I'm not accusing you of anything. We're just talking." Laredo let him go. "It would be possible for someone to do that, wouldn't it?"

Stella glowered. He was probably not used to losing fights, Laredo thought.

Laiksen jumped in. "I think they come in a wagon and left in a wagon. What you figger, Hank?"

Stella nodded. "Think they did."

Laiksen said, "T'other would be too goddam complicated. And there'd be a trail—I mean you'd have to have men to move them guns. They heavy as hell."

"How many men could do it?" Laredo asked. "There were six boxes. Three of ammunition."

"Weighs like hell, ammunition does."

Stella said, "Maybe four men."

"Not two?"

Stella shrugged. "Depends . . . two men'd take a lot longer."

"That's right," Laiksen said quickly. "They come and went wi'out losing no time. They was three guards on duty at the main gate that night. They take turns makin' rounds.

12

These fellas, they come in and left while the third man was still on his rounds."

"How long on the rounds?"

"Maybe an hour."

Laredo pinched his lower lip. "Maybe that just happened—I mean coming and going while one man was on the rounds. It would be almost impossible for an outsider to know when the man was on the rounds, wouldn't it?"

Laiksen nodded. "I told them special *not* to make the rounds at regular times."

Laredo smiled. "Well, we've learned something, gents. I'm sure Mr. Stella is right—there were four men. I believe it's most likely they came and went in their own wagon. Now the question is—where did they go?"

Chapter Three

LAREDO interviewed the two clerks that afternoon. One was the chief clerk, Matt Hewitt, the other one of the staff, Jonas Peel.

Hewitt was a tall, solemn man with gray hair and a rather condescending manner. He dressed well and obviously considered himself one of the elite. He had answered the federal detectives' questions, he told Laredo, and was not particularly eager to go through it all again.

Laredo met him in Hewitt's ordered office and closed the door, showing his credentials. "I'm interested in knowing, Mr. Hewitt, how the robbers knew the Gatlings were in that particular boxcar."

"I cannot tell you."

"Mr. Laiksen informs me that four people knew. You are one of them. Could anyone else have had access to the records?"

"Perhaps—if they knew where to look."

"What do you mean?"

"I mean, we do not let our private records lie about. They are very carefully put under lock and key and the filing system is of my own devising."

"It's a code of some sort?"

"Rather in that direction, yes. The average person would have no idea how to trace a particular record."

"But Mr. Peel knew . . ."

"Yes, because he was working on that specific shipment. No other of the clerks knew, because it was not necessary that they knew."

"How long were the guns here at Pendleton?"

"A total of two and a half days."

Laredo was surprised. It meant quick work for someone to pass the news along. "Did you know of the shipment before it arrived?"

Hewitt paused, frowning at him. "Yes," he said finally. "I knew it was due."

"In advance?"

"Yes, a day or so in advance."

"Did Mr. Peel know that?"

"No, he did not."

"May I speak to Mr. Peel, please?"

Hewitt nodded. "You can speak to him here. I'll send him in."

"Thank you."

Hewitt went out and in a few moments a short, dumpy man entered. He was pale, overweight and shabbily dressed in comparison with Hewitt. He said, "You wanted to see me? I'm Jonas Peel."

"Yes. Sit down, Mr. Peel. This is about the Gatlings."

"I don't know anything about those damn guns!"

"You knew they were in that boxcar."

"So did other people!"

Laredo smiled. "You're not being accused of anything, Mr. Peel. I assume you don't have a guilty conscience . . ."

"Of course not!"

"I'm sure you have handled valuable merchandise many times before and have not stolen any of it. . . ."

"I never see the merchandise. All I see are the papers. And I don't usually know what's in the boxes or crates. Those Gatlings happened to be government property."

"Where were they bound for?"

"New Orleans, if I remember."

Peel had cooled down a bit but was still edgy. Was it very likely that a man like Peel would know the kind of men who could steal important merchandise and kill a guard doing it? No, it was not.

He asked a few more questions and let Peel go. When Hewitt returned to the office Laredo asked, "Have there been other similar robberies in the last year or so?"

"No. Nothing like this one. There are always cases of petty theft—or mislaid articles, but nothing of any importance."

"I see . . ." He thanked Hewitt for his time and went out to the buggy. One of those four had talked. He was sure of it. Someone had paid well for information. And who needed money—was it little dumpy Peel? Didn't his kind always need money?

He drove to the livery and turned over the buggy, saying he would be back for it in the morning. He had supper in a restaurant in the city. The men who had committed the crime were obviously ruthless, ready to kill. Maybe too ready. Could they be small-time thugs hired to do this job? It was entirely possible they had been given the information and told exactly how and when to do the robbery . . . maybe.

He ate a steak with boiled potatoes, drank a cup of coffee, thinking about it. There were conflicting things about the job, he thought. It had been well planned but it had been carried out by men ready to kill—thugs. Had the planner intended that the guards be killed? Four men ought to have been able to overpower and tie them up.

Laredo went back to the hotel with a newspaper. With any kind of luck the man in the hospital would be able to tell him something of the four.

The man in the tiny four-bed hospital was Nyall Rozak, a big, burly man who looked out of place on the cot despite his bandages. Laredo introduced himself and drew up a chair

16

as the nurse cautioned him to remain only a few moments. Rozak was conscious, but looked as if his eyes did not focus.

Laredo asked, "How many men were there?"

"Four," Rozak said, barely forming the word. His head was heavily bandaged and the room smelled of medicine.

"It was midnight. Wasn't that an odd time to be picking up the crates?"

"Yes . . ." Rozak seemed to want to say more and Laredo waited. In a moment he said, "Uniforms."

"They wore uniforms?"

"Y-yes."

"What kind of uniforms—army?"

"No. Pen-l-ton."

Laredo leaned closer. "You mean they wore Pendleton overalls?"

"Y-yes."

"Ahh. So you thought they worked for the company!"

Rozak seemed to smile. "Yes." He closed his eyes.

Laredo said, "You've been a big help, Mr. Rozak." The burly man opened and closed his eyes.

The nurse said, "That's all, Mr. Garrett. He's very weak."

Laredo rose at once. "I'll come back later. Thank you."

He went out into the sunshine to peer at the sky. So there had been four men, and they had been wily enough to wear Pendleton uniforms to allay suspicions of the men at the gate. That meant planning had gone into the raid, over and above acquiring the information about the guns.

When he went back to the hotel, Pete Torres was there, grinning at him, white teeth in a brown face. Pete was a stocky man, dark and black-eyed, with a quick intelligence and the strength of an oak tree. "How the hell are you, *amigo*?"

"Eking out a living." They embraced. Pete had arrived an hour past, he said, and had had a bath while waiting for Laredo to show up.

17

"The wire didn't say anything much," Pete said. "What'ave we got here?"

"Robbery. A valuable cargo lifted, and one murder."

"The last time we worked together it was murder. People keep shooting each other."

Laredo shrugged. "A quick way to solve problems—they think. The last one we worked on was about cows. This is about Gatling guns."

"I read something about it in the papers." Pete pulled out the makin's and slipped out a brown paper. "I remember we fired Gatlings at Barksdale, but I never thought I'd see one again."

"Let's hope we see 'em again. We've got to recover the guns."

They walked to the saloon nearby and sat at a corner table with beer steins in front of them while Laredo filled Pete in.

Pete said, "Four of them knew about the guns, huh? Which one do you pick?"

"I think one of the clerks is most likely, but I'm not sure exactly why I think so."

"Why not the manager or the yard boss?"

"Maybe a hunch. I don't see either of them as a killer." Laredo shrugged. "Or going along with a killing. Those four intended to kill Rozak too. He was just lucky."

"And the clerks are well out of the action?"

"Yes. They probably didn't know the guards, but Laiksen and Stella did. That kind of thing can make a difference."

Torres sipped beer. "What about the wagon they used?"

"That was my next project. If these four were thugs hired to do the job, is it likely they had a wagon along with them?"

"Hell no. They got one here."

"That's what I think. We'll have to visit all the livery stables in town. But just for the report we'll have to look in on Laiksen and Stella off-duty." He pulled a coin from his pocket. "Which one do you want?"

"I'll take Stella."

"Call it in the air." Laredo flipped the coin, caught it and plopped it onto the table under his hand as Pete said, "Heads."

He lifted the hand. "Heads it is. You get Stella." He pocketed the coin. "We'll find out where he and Laiksen live from the office records."

They got that information the next day, as well as the home addresses of Matt Hewitt and clerk Peel.

It took only two hours that day to discover the wagon used in the robbery. It had been rented from the stable of old Jody Thrasher. It had been rented by a single man one afternoon and returned that night late.

"You stay open all night?" Pete asked Jody.

"Naw. He left the wagon in front with the team."

"What did he look like?"

"Ornery-looking cuss. But he paid good money. Left 'is horse in the corral."

"Not much," Laredo said when they had left. "But now we're sure they were an out-of-town bunch and there were four of them. The next question is: where did they go?"

Pete rolled a brown cigarette. "They must have left the Pendleton yard about one in the morning. Four men in a light wagon with six crates."

"Probably covered."

"Yes. But a goddam unusual sight for one in the morning. Did they go into town?"

"I doubt it."

Pete nodded. "Me, too. Let's look at a map."

They found one at the hotel and spread it out on a table in Laredo's room. It showed the city of Lockhart, the railroad line, a dozen roads, and the river.

"The river," Laredo said, putting his finger on it. "A natural getaway in a boat. The robbery was well planned, why not plan the getaway too?"

"Of course." Pete's finger traced a route from the Pendleton yard to the river. "No houses along here—they had

19

the road to themselves at that hour and they could have turned off the road to the river in several places. They had a boat waiting.''

"We're doing a lot of guessing . . ."

Pete grinned. "We're good guessers. I bet you a month's pay they're in some river town right now with those guns.''

"You're such a good guesser, you guess which one.''

Pete sighed. "Yeah . . . which one?''

Chapter Four

Both Laredo and Pete Torres had passes from the manager, Laiksen, so they were able to move in and out of the Pendleton yard at will. It was thus easy to wait for Laiksen to leave the yard to go home . . . and to follow him.

Pete followed Stella.

Neither of the two men met anyone outside the yard, and both went directly home each time they were tailed. Laredo and Pete discussed it after three days.

"Either they know we're following them or they're clean," Pete said.

"Or there's no job planned."

Pete shrugged.

"All right. Let's switch over to the two clerks." Laredo flipped a coin again and Pete won Jonas Peel.

In three days they met again to discuss the situation. Neither of the clerks had met anyone or done anything out of the ordinary. Innocence abounded.

Laredo said, "I vote we do what the other detectives did."

"What's that?"

"Give up on the case."

"What?"

Laredo grinned. "We announce that the case is probably one of those that will never be solved, and that we're going on to other things. We'll say we've been ordered off the case."

Pete nodded. "So we leave town—then come back."

"Exactly."

"I like it."

The next day Laredo met Laiksen in his office. He said, "I have to report that we've been pulled off the case, Tim."

Laiksen was surprised. "I thought you made some headway."

"Not enough. Our bosses want us somewhere else. They say this case will probably never be solved. It was done by professionals and they're long gone . . . maybe even in Europe by now."

"Hmm. Well, I'm sorry. That damned robbery reflects on the company. I wanted to see them caught."

"Me, too." They shook hands and Laredo departed. He mentioned to the gate guards that he and Torres were called off the case, that it was unsolvable. He was sure the gossip would spread.

That morning, near noon, they took the train in Lockhart and rode to the next stop. And got off forty miles away.

Laredo spent a half hour in the telegraph office composing a coded message to John Fleming in Washington, telling him what he and Pete were doing, asking Fleming to send a wire to Laiksen thanking him for his cooperation, and saying he was sorry the case had to be terminated.

"That'll nail it down."

They bought horses and saddles, dressed in jeans and boots and set out for Lockhart again. Taking pains to look like drifters, they arrived in the city late and put up at a cheap boardinghouse only a mile or so from the Pendleton warehouse.

Again flipping a coin, they chose Matt Hewitt as their first suspect. He was unmarried and lived in a well-kept boardinghouse in a better part of the city.

It was child's play to follow him home from the Pendleton gate, but the first night he did not appear again.

The second night was Friday and an hour after he entered the boardinghouse he reappeared, dressed in different clothes, got his light buggy out of the stable and drove across town.

In front of a garishly painted structure called the Fun Palace, Hewitt gave the buggy over to a hostler and went inside.

"He's a playboy!" Pete Torres said.

"Maybe he's here on business." Laredo made a face. "Give him the benefit of the doubt."

They wandered in, keeping Hewitt in sight. The clerk went into the saloon at once where he seemed to know everyone. The bartenders greeted him and several of the painted girls came to banter with him.

"What kind of business?" Pete asked.

"Maybe he does their books."

They watched Hewitt dance with several of the girls, buy them drinks, and finally take one upstairs.

Laredo asked a bartender, "What's upstairs?"

"Rooms," the man said with some surprise. "You want a room for the night? The girl'll cost you extra."

"Can I get a room without the girl?"

The barman shrugged. "I guess so. Nobody ever asked me that before."

"I'll go up and see."

Leaving Pete at the bar, Laredo went up the stairs and found a desk at the landing. A bespectacled man in a leather vest looked at him, raising his brows. "Yes?"

"You rent rooms?"

"Of course."

"That man who just came up with the girl. Do you know him?"

"Why?"

"He's a cousin of mine. Name's Johnny Beech."

The other shook his head. "You got the wrong *hombre*,

23

friend." He turned the register. There was a column of names. Hewitt had signed as Charles Barnes.

"I'll be damned," Laredo said. "He looked just like Johnny." He scratched his chin. "He been here before?"

"Plenty times."

Laredo managed a weak smile. "Well, guess I made a mistake. Sorry." He went back down the stairs, made a signal to Pete and met him outside.

"He's a regular customer here. Signed in as Charles Barnes."

"That takes money. I didn't think clerks got paid enough to throw money away on girls."

"Maybe he inherited it."

Pete grinned. "And maybe he got it selling Gatling guns."

"You have a very suspicious mind."

"I think we've found our informant. Hewitt met somebody here in the saloon and made a deal to sell information. Do you like that story?"

Laredo nodded. "I like it fine. But we'll have to check out Mr. Hewitt a little more. One fling doesn't make him a crook."

"It's a hell of an indication."

Laredo pursed his lips. "So what's your suggestion?"

"I say we take him somewhere and work him over. I think he's guilty—you tell him he's not."

"Sure. I think we'll get some names out of him—or something we can use. He's got to know *something*."

"All right. We'll intercept him next time he goes to the Fun Palace."

He went two nights later. Laredo and Torres closed in, one from each side, pointing revolvers at him and Hewitt halted in alarm. "What is this! A robbery?"

"Come along with us, Mr. Hewitt."

Hewitt recognized Laredo. "You! You're a robber!?"

24

"No. We want to ask you some questions. Turn the buggy around, please."

Hewitt's chin came up. "Ask me here."

Pete Torres said, "Turn the goddam buggy or I'll kick your ass. You hear?"

Hewitt jumped at the tone. He slapped the reins viciously, turning the horse, glaring at Torres. "You have no right to do this!"

"Do as we tell you," Laredo said patiently.

They had picked out an old barn, half tumbled down and gray with age, the shake roof mostly gone. Weeds as tall as a man grew everywhere; no one had visited the place for years. It was far off the traveled road, and they took Hewitt there. By the time he arrived he was shaken and pale, all the bravado squeezed out of him.

Pete pulled him out of the buggy and he fell to his knees, making small sounds in his throat. Immediately Laredo helped him up.

"Don't be so rough, Emilio. Mr. Hewitt is going to tell us what we want to hear." He brushed Hewitt's clothes with his hand. "Aren't you, Mr. Hewitt?"

Pete slid a gleaming knife from his belt. "Just gimme two minutes with him. I'll find out—" He stepped toward Hewitt menacingly.

Laredo pushed him away, moving between them. "Just tell us what you know about the robbery, Mr. Hewitt."

"I don't know a thing! You've got the wrong man!"

Laredo said gently. "We think you know a great deal. Tell us and you can go home unharmed."

"I told you—I don't know a thing!"

Laredo shrugged as if in defeat; he looked at Pete. "Well, I'm afraid he's not going to cooperate."

Pete brandished the glittering knife. "All right, now it's my turn." He grabbed at Hewitt who scuttled away, squealing in terror.

"Keep him off me! Keep him off me!" He tripped over his own foot and flopped on the ground.

Pete grabbed one leg and pulled him back. Making a terrible face, he lifted the knife high—and Hewitt shrieked and fainted.

Laredo let his breath out in disgust. "Pour some water on him."

Pete got a canteen off the horse and poured a liberal splash on the clerk who sputtered and mewed and opened his eyes weakly.

Laredo knelt by him, holding the man's arm tightly. In a very serious voice he said: "You're not cut bad, Hewitt. I don't think you'll lose much blood—but you'll have to lie still."

Hewitt's mouth fell open and he spied Pete who was wiping the knife blade. He yelped and struggled and Laredo held him tightly. "I told you to lie still!"

"I want a doctor!"

"It'll take you an hour or so to bleed to death, Hewitt. Unless you want us to bandage you . . ."

"Oh yes, yes, yes, bandage me!"

"Then tell us about the robbery."

Hewitt moaned.

Pete said, "Lemme cut him again, a little deeper."

"No! No, no, no!" Hewitt cried and began to pant, his arms thrashing. "I'll tell you—I'll tell you!"

"That's good," Laredo said smiling. "Put the knife away, Emilio. He's going to cooperate after all."

Chapter Five

"**A**LVY Bowen!" Hewitt said, gasping. "He's the one."

"There were four of them," Laredo told him.

"Alvy was the one I met—I don't know about the others."

"Where did you meet him?"

"At the Fun Palace, months ago. I went there now and then to have a beer."

Pete said, "Months ago?"

Hewitt was getting a bit of nerve back, but he was still wary of Pete. "He came to me with an offer of money . . . talked a lot about the girls I could have if I had money in my jeans. He wanted information—wanted to know when a good score came up."

"And when you heard the Gatlings were coming, you told him?"

"Yes. I received word about them a week or so before they arrived." He looked at Laredo. "What're you going to do with me?"

"We'll have to turn you in."

"But I helped you!"

"Where can we find Alvy Bowen?"

"I don't know. He never told me anything." He saw Torres pull out the knife again and yelled: "I don't know! I'm telling you the truth!"

"Get in the buggy," Laredo said. "We'll take you back to town."

Hewitt had discovered he hadn't been cut. His clothes were wet from the canteen, but he was unharmed. Grumpily he climbed into the buggy.

They took him to the city police and preferred charges.

They had a name, Alvy Bowen, and laid it in front of the local captain. "Do you know this man?"

The captain, a grizzled veteran, nodded quickly. "He's a small-time crook with a record of armed robbery and various holdups. He's a no-good. Why do you ask?"

"We think he was one of the four who robbed Pendleton."

The captain whistled. "Then you think Alvy is the one who got Hewitt into it?"

"Yes. Hewitt's admitted it. Where can we find Bowen?"

"Probably somewhere along the river. I doubt if he's ever had a permanent address. That's about all I can tell you."

Laredo smiled. "It's more than we knew before."

Somewhere along the river.

"Not much to go on," Pete said. "We'll have to start asking folks."

The nearest river town was Newburg and they headed for it early in the morning, a bright crystal-clear day that gradually turned cloudy as they approached the river. Newburg was small, only a single main street parallel with the river and a long levee with thick tree-bole piles driven into the gray mud along a several hundred foot front. Dirt had been packed in behind the piles and the top of the levee was floored with rough, heavy planks. Several dozen small boats were moored alongside it.

The town had a dingy hotel with a horsestall-sized area with a desk behind which was a bespectacled oldster who greeted them in a quavery voice. There were five rooms available, the old man said, though he expected to rent three the next day. Laredo signed for two, then they went along the street to a restaurant in an unpainted building and ate ribs and lima beans with bitter-tasting coffee.

When they paid for the meal they asked about a man named Alvy Bowen, but the proprietor shook his head and told them he'd never heard the name.

They asked the same question in the town's three saloons, but no one could tell them a thing except that definitely Alvy did not live in the town.

"It means he never robbed anyone here," Pete said. "Do we go upriver or down?"

Laredo rubbed his chin. "If you were in a hurry, which way would you go?"

"Down."

"You bet. That's the way I vote too."

According to the old man behind the hotel desk, the next river town was a half-day's ride south, and they took the narrow track after breakfast. The clouds had increased, making the day shadowy, and a chill wind came sweeping off the river, causing them to button their coats tightly.

The next town was Ferris, and they arrived cold and tired. It was a burg not much larger than Newburg, but built back from the river on a high bank. The first bartender they asked had heard of Alvy Bowen.

"Don't know the *hombre*, but heard the name—think I seen it on a poster too."

"You probably did."

"Umm. Thought he was in jail."

"Yeh, he was."

29

"He run with a no-good name of Clete. I forgit his last handle. You gents Pinkertons? What's he done now?"

"We're not Pinkertons," Pete said. "A friend of ours got dead and we want to talk to Alvy about it."

"Where d'you figure we could find him?" Laredo asked.

The barman shook his head. "Them types keeps moving. He could be anywhere."

Ferris had no hotel so they made a bargain with the livery-stable owner, put their horses in stalls and slept in an empty area. In the morning they had breakfast and put the town behind them.

The country turned flat and open for miles; the river meandered wide and serene, bending southeast, and the weather cleared. It was warm when they came into Corvis, a large town on the stageline. They got down in front of the New Alamo Saloon, went inside and ordered beer.

The room was nearly deserted. Two men stood talking quietly at the end of the bar and a single older man was playing solitaire at a table. Laredo asked the bartender, "You know a man named Alvy Bowen?"

The men at the end of the bar stopped talking and looked at him. The oldster at the table turned his head to stare. The bartender frowned. "Heard of him."

"Everybody has," Laredo said pleasantly, glancing at the others. "Is he in town?"

"Sure as hell hope not," the bartender said, wiping the bar with a rag. "You friends of his'n?"

"Not particularly," Pete remarked. "Where's a good place to look for him?" He included everyone in his question.

The barman asked, "You police or Rangers?"

"Just interested parties," Laredo said. "We have a bone to pick with him."

"I reckon plenty has," the barman said. "Alvy's a holdup man, you know. I figgered he was still in jail."

30

"He's out," Pete said, finishing the beer.

One of the men at the end of the bar spoke up. "You gents know Billy Hatcher?"

Laredo shook his head.

"Billy got a harness shop down t'other end of town. Knows all the gossip. He better'n a newspaper. You ast him about Alvy."

"Thanks." Laredo waved and they went out and climbed on the horses.

The harness shop was little more than a large shed. It had a dirt floor and harnesses hanging everywhere. The barnlike door was open and the place smelled strongly. They left the horses at the hitchrack and went inside, wrinkling their noses.

They found Billy in the back, sitting on a box, half drunk. He looked at them owlishly. "Howdy, gents . . ." He tried to get up and failed. "Wha' kinda day is it?"

"Nice day," Laredo said. There was a bottle near Billy's hand and he moved it out of reach. The room had a cot bed, some old clothes hanging from a line, a grimy window, a pitcher and basin that looked unused and several boxes that were apparently used as chairs. He sat down on one. Pete stood by the door.

"You come f'sometin'?" Billy asked.

"We came about Alvy Bowen."

"A-Alvy?"

"That's right. Alvy Bowen."

Billy hiccuped. "He a holdup man." He tried to focus on Laredo. "Wha' you want wi' him?"

"Where can we find him?"

Billy considered the question, blinking his eyes. "Alvy B-Bowen?"

"Yes."

"Heard Alvy was in pri-pr-prison."

"He was but he's out now. Where can we find him?"

Billy shook his head slowly and closed his eyes. He took

31

a deep breath and tried to focus on Laredo again. "Thass right. He out now. I 'member. Didju ast his wife?"

"Alvy's got a wife?"

Billy nodded ponderously. "What I heard. Married some girl in Humbolt."

"What's Humbolt?"

Billy chuckled. "F'crissake, it's a town . . ." He felt for the bottle.

Pete said, "Let's get outta here. Smells like hell!"

Laredo moved the bottle back and got up. "Thanks, Billy." They hurried out to the hitchrack, taking deep breaths of fresh air.

Humbolt, they found, was a town not far downriver. The river made a wide bend but the road cut across, saving many miles.

They rode in slowly. It was a mean little town, far gone to seed. It was set back from the river with a swath of swampy land between. Laredo could see several brown water areas where boats had been pushed in through reeds from the river and were pulled up on the muddy bank. One or two had masts, and fishing tackle hung up to dry.

It was quiet, almost silent except for a few wheeling birds. A vagrant breeze trailed through nearby pine tops. A few expressionless faces watched them as they entered one end of the town and stopped at a hitchrack where there was a watertrough.

Laredo rubbed his nose. "Feels like a funeral."

"Yeh. The town's dead." Pete stepped down and hitched up his belt. He slid both arms over the saddle seat and gazed around. "Dead as a horseshoe nail. Why would anybody live here?"

Laredo got down. "To dodge the law."

"Umm. I expect you're right. There's probably no law within a hundred miles. D'you think we look prosperous?"

"I hope not." Laredo eased the Colt revolver in its holster. "But travelers usually have a dollar or two."

"Alvy Bowen's one of *them*. We'd best not be too curious about him."

"We could say he's a cousin."

Pete glanced at him. "How's that sound to you?"

"It could be better. What if we're supposed to meet him here?"

"And what if he's already here?"

"Well, you think of something."

Pete considered. "The panhandle isn't too far. We could be a couple of hardcases from Texas . . . drifting through."

"Not bad. We're three jumps ahead of a sheriff?"

"Well . . . five maybe. We don't want to make anyone nervous."

Clete was edgy and so was Alvy and the others. They were all restless with the waiting. They had been at Grannie's place too long. The days were slipping by. . . .

Getts's letter had come a week past. A drummer had picked it up with a sack of mail and delivered it to Karl Boise in the saloon in Humbolt. It was addressed to Clete Anderson in care of the Two Barrels.

Getts was delayed. He had been implicated in a shooting and had been detained as a witness until the circuit judge appeared. "Sit tight," the letter said. "I will be there as soon as I can get away. The judge is due in two days."

More waiting.

Grannie went into Humbolt every week and bought supplies and came back with the weekly newspaper which they pored over. The first papers weeks ago had been full of the robbery and murder. The law had no clues and the hurt man was still alive but with a fractured skull.

But the last two papers had barely mentioned the Pendleton affair. Probably the police had given it up, Clete said. No one had followed them. Fred Orne had been back a long time and no one had followed him either. How long were they going to wait for Getts?

All Grannie had was cider but there was whiskey in town—and girls. Alvy went in often to see one particular girl. She seemed to regard him as something more than just a customer. . . .

And ten days crawled by.

Chapter Six

THE saloon had no name, merely a sign with two barrels painted on it. They went inside the dark and not a little smelly place and ordered whiskey. There was a sign over the bar: NO BEER TODAY.

The man behind the bar was fat and greasy with almost no hair and puffy eyes. He served them reluctantly, took their money and moved away. There was no one else in the room. Laredo sipped the drink and pushed it away. It was the worst whiskey he had ever tasted.

He said loudly, "We looking for an old friend of ours, Alvy Bowen. You know 'im?"

The barman stared at him. "Mebbe."

"What's that mean, maybe? You know 'im or not?"

Pete moved down the bar so that they were separated. The barman looked from one to the other of them. "Where you know Alvy from?"

"Texas," Laredo said. He indicated Pete. "Three of us did a little business down there. What town was that, Emilio?"

"Don't remember," Pete said. "We got out too goddam fast."

"Yeah, we did. Where's Alvy now, friend?"

The barman shook his head. "Ain't got any idea."

"You seen him lately?"

"No."

Laredo nodded. This man was too suspicious for much more. If they pushed him he would probably lie to them. He walked down the bar to the door.

Pete followed him out and they stood in the street as Pete rolled a cigarette. "I got a hunch Alvy's here."

"I think so too . . . in this area anyway. Wonder if the other three are with him?"

Pete struck a match. "Whose theory was it that they were paid to do the job? Maybe they had to deliver the goods."

"They could have delivered the crates long ago."

"Yeh." Pete puffed and looked at the cigarette.

Humbolt had no hotel and the livery stable owner would not allow them to bed down in a stall. They bought a tarpaulin in the general store, as well as some food which they put in a sack, and rode into the trees at the end of town. They would have to camp out, but after the rigorous training at the Tanner Barksdale training center, neither man noticed any hardship. At Barksdale they had been put through courses as tough and demanding as sadistic minds could devise and both had come through with flying colors.

They dug a pit and made a tiny fire, broiled meat and covered the fire. Pete smoked a cigarette as they gazed through the trees at the distant lights of the little town. It was very likely, Laredo thought, that Humbolt was Alvy Bowen's hangout—or one of them. But how to get to Alvy? They had one other name: Clete. So far it wasn't doing them much good.

In the morning they decided to return to the town. "We're drifters," Laredo said. "We'll drift in and see what's happening. We could get lucky."

"I hope we don't have to drink much of that miserable whiskey. . . ."

Alvy Bowen entered the saloon in the middle of the evening, bent on seeing one of the girls, preferably Lacy. There

36

were three who hung out at the Two Barrels and Lacy was the prettiest. When he was away from Humbolt he often told people he was married to her. It kept him warm on chilly nights, thinking he was.

Lacy was upstairs, busy with someone, so he sat at the bar and talked to Karl. Karl said, "Couple friends o' yours in here t'day."

"Yeh? They have handles?"

"Didn't say. Said they did some business with you down in Texas."

Alvy frowned. "I never been in Texas."

"You sure?"

"Hell yes, I'm sure. I know where I been. I never been in Texas. What'd these two look like?"

"They looked like drifters. Wait a minute—one of 'em was called Emilio. Looked like a Mexican."

"I don't know no Mexicans." Alvy leaned closer. "Where'd they go to?"

"I seen them go over to the store, then they rode out south."

"Thanks." Alvy finished his drink and went out. Those two could be coppers. What he had told Karl wasn't exactly true; he had been in Texas once, in the panhandle, but never did any business there and especially not with those two.

He rode back to Grannie's turning it over in his mind. And the more he thought about it the more he became convinced the two were coppers. Maybe even bounty hunters.

Somehow they had left a trail. Or Fred Orne had. But when he talked to Fred, the other said he hadn't seen anyone on the trail south, and he was positive he hadn't been followed.

"I watched my goddam backtrail. You figger I don't know how t'do that?"

Alvy blew out his breath. Yeah, Fred knew how to do it.

They all discussed it, sitting around the table with some

37

of Grannie's cider. Clete said, "We got to stay here till Huey Getts pays us off."

Ira suggested, "Hell, we could sell the guns somewheres else."

"Where? You know a buyer who got that much cash?"

"We could find one."

Clete said, with overmuch patience, "We can't advertise in the goddam papers that we got Gatling guns to sell. The federals would be all over us like fleas on Grannie's dog."

"We could put the word out quiet," Alvy said.

"It'd take too long." Clete moved his shoulders. "It makes me nervous just havin' them guns close by. The goddam federals would shove us in Leavenworth Prison and we'd never git out."

Ira growled, "I'd take 'em out in the river and sink 'em first."

Grannie moaned at the idea.

"What about them two in town?" Alvy asked. "They could disappear . . ."

Clete mused, "They're not reportin' to anybody because there ain't a telegraph wire in maybe seventy-five miles." He grinned. "Anything could happen to 'em."

"And nobody would ever know," Ira said, showing his teeth.

They had camped in a tiny hollow and in the morning Laredo walked down the slope to an outcropping where he could get a better look at the town. A boat was pushing out through the brown swampy waters toward the river; two men were propelling it with poles. A limp sail hung from a short mast. He watched them reach the clear water and fasten the sail in place. A vagrant breeze heeled the boat over slightly and they went downstream slowly. They had the look of fishermen.

Nothing moved in the town. It had only one street, with shabby buildings on both sides and smoke trailing from a half dozen chimneys. Behind the line of storefronts were a half dozen shacks and one or two that could be called houses.

Even from a distance it had the look of a mean little burg, he thought.

Wishing he had a pair of binoculars, he peered at the boats tied up along the muddy shore. Only one or two were large enough to contain the six crates. Had the four men brought the Gatlings here?

So many questions. Were the four men still together? If they found Alvy or Clete would those two lead them to the others? Where were the damn guns?

Too many questions.

A man came out of a store and crossed the street below in a lazy slouch.

And something rattled a dry bush somewhere to his right. Laredo fell into a crouch, the Colt pistol in his hand. He could see movement down the gentle slope; several men were climbing up toward him. He saw the glint of steel from a rifle.

Bending far over, he went back to the horses. Pete was mounted, leaning over the horn. Laredo said, "We've got visitors." He swung into the saddle and turned the horse.

Pete Torres led the way. He found a gully and turned into it, spurring the animal. They galloped over the sandy bottom for a hundred yards and came to a rock face. As they climbed out of the ravine the first shots cracked past them, fired from a distance.

"Too damned eager," Pete said. "How many of 'em?"

"I only saw two . . . could be more."

"Is it Alvy and his bunch?"

Laredo grinned. "Who else? You got enemies in this part of the world?"

"Not me."

"I think we ought to split up, make it hard for them. We can meet later—"

"Just north of the town?"

"Good enough. *Suerte, amigo.*"

"*Que le vaya bien.*"

Laredo went to the left, drawing the Winchester from the boot and levering a shell into the chamber. He put the rifle across his thighs. It was a clear, not too warm day, with no wind at all. The country was rolling with high brush and clumps of trees. The pursuers would know the lay of the land, of course, but it might not help them.

He walked the horse for a hundred yards and halted in the shade of a copse of trees, lifting the rifle. He had no intention of letting them chase him. A man came into view at extreme range, crossing to his left. He was riding a roan and had a rifle resting on his thigh, muzzle in the air.

When the man disappeared, Laredo nudged the horse and moved forward, hoping to get behind them. But a second man came into view, saw Laredo and instantly fired. The shot went wild and Laredo aimed carefully and sent three shots at the man, saw his horse stagger, then a fusillade of shots came at him from the left.

None were aimed, probably designed to drive him off. Laredo spurred to the left, snapping shots in the direction of the second man with no hope of hitting him. He paused to reload the rifle, dismounted and tied the horse in a group of bushy trees and ran forward. They might not expect him on foot.

Crawling to the top of a rise, he peered over, hatless. He could see several hundred yards to his front and sides and nothing moved. He could not see the man he had fired at. What would they do now?

A buzzard climbed high in the blue a mile or so to his right and began to circle. Laredo lay perfectly still, smelling the dry grass. Three feet away a motionless lizard fixed him with beady eyes.

It was very quiet. It seemed he could feel his heart beating.

Then, to his right, a small brown bird jumped into the air and flipped away over his head. Laredo half turned onto his back, drawing the Colt pistol and thumbing back the hammer. In a moment a horseman appeared, just barely in his line of sight, to the right. The horseman was wearing a brown coat and leather chaps; he halted, peering around him, a rifle held ready across his thighs.

It was a long pistol shot and Laredo considered it. He lay without moving; his shirt and jeans blended well with the brown grass and weeds. But he was not invisible. If the horseman came closer, the man would probably spot him and have the advantage of the rifle. Laredo's rifle pointed forward and any motion to bring it around would instantly be seen.

The horseman turned his head and in a moment was joined by another. They conferred in low tones and in a moment they moved forward at a fast walk, a dozen yards apart.

They would spot him in another second. Laredo's only chance was surprise. Lifting the revolver, he fired four times. The two flung themselves to the sides and one fired into the air, startled.

Laredo scuttled over the rise, rolled and poked the rifle over the ridge, getting off two shots as the horsemen galloped away out of range. He couldn't tell if he had hit either, but he had certainly shaken them up.

He reloaded, taking deep breaths. They had been startled but probably they wouldn't quit. He ran down the slope and loped in the direction they had taken. They were sure to expect him to go the opposite way.

He saw one of them again; the man was moving past a line of trees far to his right. Laredo fired two carefully aimed shots at the horse. The rider veered away instantly and it was impossible to tell if he had scored a hit. Tall brush intervened.

Laredo crawled to his right, into a narrow, brushy hollow. Lizards scuttled away as he made a nest there, arranging branches over his head, cradling the rifle. He had a clear field of fire to both sides and probably could not be seen from behind unless the viewer were almost atop him.

He remained there a long time, seeing no one else. Once he heard hoofbeats, but they went by and he did not spot the rider. Had they decided they'd had enough? Or maybe he had hurt the man badly and they'd taken him into town to get patched up.

Finally, as the sun warned him that hours had gone by, he slipped out of the nest and went back for his horse. He rode to the south, then made a wide circle to approach the town from the north. He saw no one at all.

It was a damned dangerous game they had played, but he had rather enjoyed it—though he thought his rifle was shooting a mite to the right. He ought to zero it in again when he got the chance.

Chapter Seven

IRA Page died on the way to town. He had been hit bad in the chest, knocked off his horse, and lost some blood before Clete got to him.

Clete carried him only a short distance before it was apparent Ira was gone. Clete laid him face up in the dry weeds and closed his eyes. Too bad for Ira. One share more for the rest of them.

He stayed by the body while Fred and Alvy went looking for the one who had shot Ira. They had seen two men, but one had gotten clean away. None of them were much shakes at tracking. But the second man was a bearcat.

When Fred and Alvy returned, Fred had a slash across his upper arm. The bullet had barely missed his chest, and reduced his enthusiasm for the chase considerably.

"The sonofabitch shoots good," he said.

Clete agreed. "He hit Ira from about three hunnerd yards."

They slung the body over Ira's horse and walked into town.

Ira had no kin they knew of. They weren't even sure he was using his right name. A search of his personal effects turned up nothing to help on that score. He had a pouch containing half a dozen gold eagles, a deck of cards, and an over-and-under derringer.

Clete gave one of the saloon hangers-on a gold eagle to

dig a grave in the local boot-hill and Ira was buried the next day.

Karl Boise read a page out of the Good Book and included a few remarks about a horse he had for sale and they all went back to the saloon and spent the rest of Ira's money.

After dark they rode back to Grannie's place, drunk as they could get.

Laredo and Pete Torres met just before dark a mile from the town and compared notes. Pete had not been pursued at all, and had not gone far. He had heard the gunfire and had been very concerned . . . and relieved when he saw Laredo in one piece and grinning.

"Think I hit one."

"How many chased you?"

"I saw three."

"Does that mean all four of them are here together? If they are what does *that* mean?"

Laredo shrugged. "It helps the theory that they did it for pay. And they haven't been paid yet."

"I'd say it wasn't likely." Pete shook his dark head. "They planned the robbery well, but now everything's falling apart?"

"It doesn't add up, does it?"

"Well, facts are facts. At least three of them are here. But where the hell are the Gatlings?"

"Wouldn't the guns be where they are?"

Pete smiled. "Now *that's* a smart idea. Why didn't I think of it! You mean they're staying somewhere they can keep the guns."

"It's a good guess."

"Then they're not staying at the hotel in town."

"No." Laredo rubbed his nose. "We figured they put them on a boat. I still think that was a damn good guess. Could they have brought those six crates this far in a wagon?"

"Not in a thousand years. I agree if they're here, they came by boat. It's the only thing that makes sense."

"Then let's start looking for the boat."

"It'll be guarded . . ."

Laredo nodded. "Or well hidden. Maybe both."

Pete rolled a cigarette, licked it, and felt for a match. "How do we start?"

"Well, we could ride down the riverbank—but we could ride into an ambush. Why don't we get a boat and examine the shore from it?"

"Pretending to be fishermen?" He lit the cigarette.

"Good idea. All we'll need is a canoe."

"I suggest we do it early in the morning. My grandaddy said that's when the fish bite best."

"And our friends might still be asleep." Laredo glanced around. "Let's find a place to hole up."

"First we'd better find a boat. You don't figure we're going to be able to rent one, do you?"

Laredo grinned. "We'll have to borrow one."

They found several boats drawn up out of the water at the riverbank; all had paddles in them and none were hidden. Laredo said, "They don't fear thieves."

"They don't know us," Pete replied.

They holed up in a draw a half mile from the river, spent the night and left the horses there in the morning. They put one of the smallest boats in the water and got in gingerly. Neither was used to such craft, but they quickly got the hang of it.

By the time the sun was up they were paddling slowly past the town. They were surprised to see, from the river, that there were many more houses and shacks than they'd supposed. Some were at the water's edge and each had a boat or two tied up. A few of the boats were large enough, Laredo thought, to hold the six crates.

It made the problem a little more complex.

They drifted several miles downriver, until there were no

45

more shacks to be seen. They nudged the boat to the shore. Pete rolled a brown cigarette and lit it. "That didn't get us much."

"We'd have to investigate each one of those boats. How would we do that?"

"Swim to them."

Laredo made a face. "There's one thing we can't forget."

"What's that?"

"We are dealing with killers. Any one of those men would kill us on suspicion alone."

"And besides, that water is cold as hell. Let's think of something else." He puffed on the cigarette. "What if we wait around till someone comes for the guns?"

"How would we know?"

"Well, it'd have to be a bigger boat."

Laredo sighed. "How many places can you be at the same time? This is a long river. Besides, it wouldn't have to be another boat. Why couldn't they use the boat the guns are in now?"

"If they're in a boat."

"Yeh," Laredo said grumpily. "We don't know a hell of a lot."

They returned upriver, paddling to the far side and moving up out of the current. It took a much longer time to return to the place they'd "borrowed" the boat. They left it and went back to the horses, feeling discouraged.

Pete said, "What if we wired the home office and asked for help?"

"You mean get more men? What would we do with them?"

"Round up Alvy and the bunch."

"Oh. You know where they are?"

Pete grunted.

Laredo said, "I'm going into the town tonight and see what I can find."

"They're killers . . ."

46

"Yes, but we won't learn anything sitting out here in the sticks."

"You can't go in any saloon in town. They'll know you're a stranger. They'll grab you and hold you for Alvy."

"I won't go into any goddam saloon."

"You're going to stand in the street and talk to yourself?"

Laredo sighed deeply. "I don't know what I'm going to do, but I'm not going to stay out here and hope one of them falls into my lap."

Pete pulled out a stack of makin's and fiddled with it. "All right, but I'm not going to let you go alone."

They left the horses a half mile from the edge of town. There was no moon and a chill mist was drifting in from the river. The town was mostly dark, only two saloons were lighted and piano music came from the Two Barrels.

The town had no boardwalk; each building was separate and had its own walk or none at all. The Two Barrels had a walk the width of the building with a half dozen chairs scattered along it—with no one occupying them. Seven horses waited at the hitchrack as well as a buckboard and a farm wagon.

Laredo stepped up onto the porch and looked over the top of the bat-wing doors. There were probably twenty people in the room, including a couple of painted women and the two bartenders.

Was Alvy or Clete among them?

If he stepped inside and asked, he would probably draw gunfire. The only good thing about the situation was that even as he did not know them by sight, neither did they know him.

Pete was in the shadows of the far side of the street. If trouble came, Pete would be the unexpected ace in the hole.

Laredo went around the side of the building. It had two stories, the upper was lighted; probably girls were working

47

there—or a high-stakes poker game could be in progress in one of the rooms.

At the back of the building was a stairway. He ran up the steps and tried the door at the top. It was locked. Damn. It was probably a hall door; he could see light along the door crack—and a bar or bolt that kept it closed.

He slid a knife blade into the door crack. The bar was wood. The blade went into it and he lifted it up gently, six or seven inches, and the door opened. Laredo slipped inside and replaced the bar in its holders. He was at the end of a hallway. A half dozen doors opened off it, three were standing open; the rooms were dark. He slipped into one. It smelled of perfume or powder.

The piano music from the saloon below reached him faintly. There were voices from several of the rooms, lifted now and then in sudden laughter. Two people came out of a room, and he ducked back; they went to the stairs at the front of the building and walked down.

The woman was back in a few minutes with another man. They went into the same room and slammed the door.

Laredo walked along the hall and listened at doors. In one the couple was quarreling. The man wanted her to go with him and she yelled that all she had from him was promises.

When the man's voice came close to the door, Laredo hurried back to the dark room. In a moment the door opened and the man came out, growling curses at her. She rushed from the room, dressed in very little, shouting at him.

"Damn you, Alvy! Go on—you're nothing but promises! It's all I ever hear!" She ran back into the room and slammed the door.

Laredo got a good look at the man. So this was Alvy Bowen! There could not be two men in that little town with the name Alvy. Alvy was slim and dark, clean-shaven with a heavy jaw. He did not look prosperous.

Laredo went back the way he had come, delighted with

the night's work. He would know Alvy instantly the next time he saw him. He told Pete what he had seen and heard.

"She said he's been making her promises?" Pete grinned. "Does that mean he hasn't any money?"

"He was wearing damn poor clothes."

"So they *haven't* been paid off for the guns!"

Chapter Eight

THE eastern newspapers learned of the Gatling-guns robbery. The Pendleton company had tried to keep it under wraps but the news leaked out and the newspapers made a tremendous stink about it. There were lurid stories about the enormous firepower of such guns—especially in the wrong hands.

Questions were asked and politicians were hard-pressed to give plausible answers. Those in power apparently conferenced and issued a joint statement saying the guns were consigned to the Orient and would never be used in the western hemisphere—when they were found, of course. The high brass of the Pendleton company also issued a statement that the guns had been under tight security and that one man had been killed in the robbery and another badly wounded protecting them.

The newspapers asked what was being done to recover them and the politicians replied that every available resource of the federal government was at work on the case and that it was expected to be broken in the near future.

John Fleming's immediate superior came to see him in the smokey office, demanding information. Fleming had to admit that though he had men on the case, he had not had a report in many days.

His superior pounded the desk. ''We must have reports,

for god's sake! How do we know that anything is being done?''

Fleming shrugged. ''The telegraph is not available in the wilds, sir. The west is not a settled region, as I am sure you are well aware.''

''Then you actually do not know if your men are even alive!?''

Fleming hesitated, puffing smoke. ''They are the best, sir. The very best. They will make a report when they are able.''

''This is very disappointing, John. You know how the newspapers are crucifying us. I suggest you send out more men. We must be able to say we are bearing down on this case. By the way, who *is* handling it?''

''The Bluestar section of Tanner.''

''Ah . . . then I will tell that to those damned newspeople. It ought to shut them up for a bit.'' He went to the door.

Fleming said, ''I'd rather you didn't mention Bluestar, sir. It *is* a top-secret organization.''

''Yes, but we need the punch. We need something to take the heat off us. I'm sure you understand.'' He went out and closed the door.

Fleming chewed the cigar. ''Shit.''

Copies of the newspapers eventually came to Humbolt. They were a week or more old and they caused much unease among Clete and the others.

''They making a lot of it,'' Fred said, frowning. ''They didn't quit the investigation at all. They could be federals comin' down here any time.''

''Why would they come here?'' Clete argued.

''Somebody shot Ira, dammit! It was one of 'em! Sure.''

''It coulda been some owl-hoot got nervous. We never seen who did it.''

''Karl Boise said they was two strangers come in looking for Alvy.'' Fred put down the newspaper. ''Those two was

51

coppers. What you want to bet?'' He shook his fist. "They was probably the ones who killed Ira.''

"I don't like it any better'n you do,'' Clete said. "But we got to wait for Huey Getts.''

"Money's running out,'' Fred growled. "We never figgered to wait this long. We could do a job but there's damn poor pickins around here. How long we going to wait?''

Alvy said, "What if we go downriver to Hopkins or one of them bigger towns?''

"And leave the guns here?''

"Take 'em with us. Who's going to know? They safe on the boat.'' Alvy grinned at them. "We might even get lucky with a buyer.''

"Lissen,'' Clete said, "the day we leave here, that's the day Getts shows up. He'll be standin' here with money in his hand and we'll be off down the goddam river with them Gatlings around our necks.''

They were silent for several moments. Then Fred asked, "How much them guns worth anyways?''

"Thousands,'' Clete said. "More'n you ever seen in your life.''

"Could we sell 'em back to the government?''

Clete rolled his eyes. "You'd have more Pinkertons runnin' around looking for you than you could count. That's a goddam tricky thing to arrange. I say we wait for Getts.''

Fred made a face. "Even if it takes another month? I ain't got two half-dimes t'rub together now. We promised Grannie a share for puttin' us up. All we got is promises.''

"Jesus, amen to that,'' Alvy said with feeling. "I been hearing that from Lacy. She yelling at me about promises. Dammit, Clete, we done our part. We got the Gatlings down here. If that goddam Getts won't pay us off, I say we go downriver with 'em and see what we can do.''

"Me, too,'' Fred said. "I never been so damn poor.''

"That's two outta three, Clete,'' Alvy said. "You still going to hold out?''

Clete let out his breath. "I think it's a mistake . . ."

"Dammit, it's *doing* something! We sitting here on our asses drinkin' Grannie's cider and we can't pay for that."

Clete nodded slowly. "All right. When you want to go?"

"What about today?"

"Not in the daylight." Clete shook his head. "If those two in Karl's saloon were federals, they might be watching. We ought to shove off at night." He looked at them and they nodded.

The owner of the Two Barrels saloon did not live on the premises. They watched him lock up, long after dark, and walk to the end of the street and into a small shacky house. In a moment a lantern light shone through the windows. The man was home alone, Pete said. The house had been dark before he got there.

Laredo motioned and stepped onto the small porch and tried the door. It was not latched. Few locked house doors. He drew his pistol, glanced at Pete, and opened the door.

He was in a small square parlor that smelled musty. There was no carpet on the puncheon floor. He could hear movement at the back of the house. Karl Boise dropped a boot on the floor, then another. Laredo moved silently through a kitchen to the bedchamber door. Boise's back was to him. The man had pulled his shirt out and was unbuttoning it at the neck.

Sensing something, the man turned suddenly and stared at them. His mouth dropped open at the sight of the pistols. "What you want?"

The room had a bed that took up much of the space, a chest of drawers, and a single chair. The lantern stood on the chest. Laredo motioned to the bed. "Sit down."

Boise sat, still staring at them as if they had come from the moon. His gaze slipped sideways to a corner and Laredo saw the shotgun standing there.

Pete saw it too, picked up the shotgun and unloaded it.

53

"What you want?" Boise said again. "I don't keep no money here."

"We're well fixed," Laredo said. "We don't want money. We want information."

"About what?"

"Not about what—about who. About Alvy Bowen and the rest."

Boise stared at them, looking from one to the other. "Youall police, huh?"

Pete went around the bed to Boise's rear. Laredo pulled the chair up and sat down facing the thickset man, the revolver pointed at his belly. "Tell us about Alvy."

"I don't know nothing about him!"

Pete suddenly took hold of both of Boise's hands, yanked them together and looped heavy twine about them deftly. Boise thought to struggle but halted at Laredo's threatening motion. In a moment his hands were securely tied behind him; he began to sweat.

Laredo said again, "Tell us about Alvy."

Boise's tone changed. "All's I know he and them others come to town. I never worked with them."

"That's not good enough, friend. You know more than that. Tell us about Clete."

Boise almost shouted, "I tell you anything and they going to kill me!"

Laredo smiled. "You are a no-good. You think we care about what happens to you? You tell us or *we'll* kill you."

Pete said, pulling his knife, "Let me at him for three or four minutes."

Laredo shrugged. "You want to talk now, don't you, friend?"

Boise stared at the glittering knife blade. "You're not going to cut me!"

"He's right," Laredo said. "Let's not cut him. Take his socks off." He smiled at Boise and Pete pulled off one of the dirty socks and held the man's leg.

54

Laredo scratched a match.

Boise yelled as Laredo passed the match flame under the foot. Sweat was rolling down his face as Boise yanked at his leg, held in an iron grip by Pete. Laredo passed the flame under the foot again, slower.

"All right!" Boise yelled. "Stop it! Stop it!"

"What about Clete and Alvy?" Laredo asked.

Boise took a long breath. He was panting heavily. "They kill me if you tell 'em . . ."

Laredo said, "We're not going to waste any more time on you. You tell us what you know or we'll burn your goddam foot off." He struck another match.

"All right!" Boise went limp. "They stayin' with Grannie, down around the curve, south. They three of 'em now. Ira got shot t'other day." He glowered at Laredo. "I 'spect you fellers did it."

"Of course," Laredo said. "So he's dead?"

Boise nodded. "Buried him."

"Who's Grannie?"

"He's a old coot. Used to be a holdup man but too old f'that now."

"We heard Alvy was married."

"Naw. He spends money on Lacy, but she don't give a damn f'him one way or other. But he ain't got any money now."

"Why not?"

"They ain't been paid for the job they did. Askin' me for credit . . ."

"Why haven't they been paid?"

Boise shook his head. "They ain't told me, but they waiting for somebody. I heard Clete say it."

"About the job they did. Do you know what it was?"

"Don't you know?"

Laredo nodded. "Do you?"

"They closemouthed. No."

"So they're all staying together at Grannie's?"

Boise nodded. "It's a house by the river, just around the bend."

Laredo looked at Pete who shook his head.

Pete cut the bonds and Boise rubbed his wrists, watching them warily. Laredo said pleasantly, "If we find out that any of your answers are wrong, we'll be back."

Boise flopped back on the bed and closed his eyes.

Outside, they walked to the horses and Pete said, "What if he hadn't talked?"

"I'd have let you cut him."

Pete chuckled. "We're getting to be a couple of *muy malo hombres.*"

"What are we dealing with?"

"Killers. That's right. They're more *malo* than we are."

Laredo swung up. "Let's go visit Grannie."

Chapter Nine

A RECONNAISSANCE on foot was in order. Laredo said, "They're sure to shoot at anyone coming close, and to ask questions later."

Pete asked, "What are the chances of Boise getting word to them that we're coming?"

"If he does, he has to tell them he's talked to us. So he won't."

They made a circle around the town and left the horses well back from the river. It was very late when they moved close to the house around the bend, watching for a dog.

Laredo crept down close to the river, looking for a boat. There was a boathouse of sorts, a kind of pier and a small inlet, but no boat. And no dog. Was the house deserted? Pete thought the chimney felt warm.

Forty feet from the house was a privy with the door standing open. They took up station in the underbrush where they could keep the door of the house and the privy in sight.

An hour after daylight an older man came from the house, slouched to the privy, pulling on a shirt, as a small dog wandered around the yard and then went back into the house with the man.

No one else came out.

"They're gone," Pete said. "We missed 'em."

"Damn." Laredo sighed. "Well, we'll have to go and talk to Grannie."

They got up and moved to the house warily, keeping out of sight of the door. But as Laredo approached the steps, the old man came out of the house holding a double-barreled shotgun. He looked as if he knew how to use it. Laredo halted.

Grannie said, "Who're you?"

"Pilgrims," Laredo said quickly. He put up his hands. "We mean no harm."

"You lost?" Grannie looked very suspicious. "How'd you git here?"

"We saw the house. We came up from the south looking to cross the river."

"Where's your hosses?"

Laredo pointed. "Around the house. Is there any way we can get across?"

"They's a town thataway." Grannie motioned to the north. "Somebody'll take you."

"All right. Thanks." Laredo moved back. The old man was watchful as hell; there was no chance to get under his guard. He and Pete walked to the horses, out of sight of the house.

"He's an old holdup man all right," Pete said. "That was quick thinking about getting across the river."

"I had to say something he'd believe. I think he was itching to pull that trigger."

Pete grunted. "Well, we're going to get nothing out of him. What's next? We go downriver?"

"We have to follow the guns. They were probably there in that inlet all the time."

"We don't even know what kind of a boat it was."

They headed south, keeping the river on their left and in a few miles found a road of sorts that paralleled the river but not close to it.

Late in the afternoon they came to a town that nestled on

the riverbank, but every boat in sight was small. They bought food supplies and kept moving. Laredo composed in his mind a report to John Fleming. They would send it at the first telegraph opportunity.

Of course it was an educated guess that the thieves were moving downstream. There was no large town upstream and no railroad connection. It did not seem sensible for them to go in that direction. The river eventually flowed into the Mississippi, and far downstream was New Orleans. Anything was possible in New Orleans, Laredo thought.

It was possible the thieves had been paid off and were now delivering the guns.

But where?

According to the map, the next large town was Hopkins, population about five thousand. Big enough, Pete said, for the robbers to lose themselves in it.

Would the search stop there? Laredo sighed inwardly. It might be time to light a candle to Lady Luck. They might well need all the help she could give them.

Clete Anderson was very unhappy about the move. In his mind it was a big mistake. They were moving from a sure thing to guesswork, but he could not convince them.

Both Alvy and Fred were getting the shakes. Inaction was eating at them; they had learned in the past that to keep moving was to stay out of jail. A sheriff's jurisdiction only went so far. And the two of them were convinced, because of the shooting of Ira, that they were being followed. Clete argued in vain that they had no evidence of it, despite the two strangers in Boise's saloon.

But they had gone downstream, got themselves stuck on a sandbar for several hours, finally pushed off it and were stranded in the shallows after rounding a bend. They stayed there the night and managed to push and tug the boat into the current again, where it swirled them around till Alvy finally got it straightened out.

They reached Hopkins at night and tied up along the long bank to wait out the dark. Fred went out and brought back a bottle and they drank it up, discussing what they would do about finding a buyer. Clete sat in a corner glowering at them. Now that they were bound downstream, he told them, they would be foolish to tell anyone what they had on board until they reached New Orleans and could deal through a broker. He knew one who would keep his mouth shut when asked.

Alvy said, "None of us're sailormen. We could sink this boat before we reach New Orleans—then where are we?"

"You takin' a bigger chance telling some goddam stranger what we got in here!" Clete yelled. "They could take it from us the same way we got it."

Fred mumbled, "Maybe we shoulda waited for Getts . . ."

Clete went out after sun-up and walked to the Planter's Hotel, after asking directions. He had told Grannie that he'd leave a letter for Getts there. Maybe Getts could catch up with them and the deal could go through as originally planned.

The hotel was seedy and ragged-looking, but he sat in the dusty lobby and laboriously wrote out a note, telling Getts what had happened and why they were here, telling him the name of the boat: *Rondo*. It was painted on the stern. He would try to make them stay a week at Hopkins, he wrote. But if they insisted on going downstream, they were eventually headed for New Orleans.

It was all he could do. He sealed the letter and wrote HUEY GETTS in large printing on the front and gave it to the clerk who dropped it into a wicker basket.

Both Fred and Alvy were sick and headachy when he returned to the boat. The bottle was empty; no one suggested moving that day.

Alvy woke in several hours in a foul mood, needing a shave. They ought to put the goddam guns on a wagon and head away from the river with them, he said. The newspapers were full of stories about the police and federal agents combing the river for them.

Clete thought he was exaggerating, but he let the other get it off his chest. Alvy went into the town looking for a place to get a bath and food. Clete sat staring at the river flowing past, thinking about the wagon. Was that such a bad idea? They could be sitting ducks on the river, and none of them knew anything about handling a boat. They might easily capsize it and lose everything. Alvy was dead right in that case.

If the federals *were* on the river looking for them, all they had to do was stop every boat going downstream and sooner or later they'd be caught.

And he had seen enough of the inside of a prison. He had sworn to himself: never again.

But if they headed into the sticks with a wagon, where would they go? How far was the Mexican border? He had no idea. But if anybody needed Gatling guns, it was Mexico.

Could three of them shepherd the guns that far, staying out of trouble? He had certain doubts.

When Alvy returned, Fred was up and growling to himself. They discussed loading the guns on a wagon. Fred said immediately, "And go where with them?"

"Anywhere to lose the pursuit," Alvy said, snapping the words out. "Hole up for a while."

Clete replied, "But we need money!"

"Then we'll do a job somewhere."

"We can't outrun a posse with those crates on our backs."

"Those damned crates!" Fred exploded. "It's always those goddam crates!"

"Well, they're here and we've got 'em," Clete said. "Getts is prob'ly sittin' with Grannie right this minute . . ."

"We hadda get out of there!" Alvy yelled. "You want to go back to prison?"

Clete growled. "There's nobody after us. How would anybody know where we went?"

"Grannie knows," Fred said with a snarl. "It wouldn't take much to make him talk."

"How would anyone know about Grannie?"

"How about Karl Boise?"

Clete shook his head. "You gettin' awful complicated. Karl won't say nothing. He don't know nothing anyway." He told them about the letter he had written and left for Getts. "He might catch up with us if we stay here for a couple days."

"Just sittin' on this goddam boat?"

"Go to a hotel then. I thought you didn't have no money!"

Alvy snapped at them. "Keep your voice down. Somebody got to stay here with the guns all the time."

Fred growled deep in his throat. "I say sell 'em to the first buyer. I dunno why the hell I ever got in this mess . . ." He climbed off the boat and disappeared to return in a short time with another bottle.

There was a waterfront restaurant not far off and Alvy and Clete went there and ate fish and bread and when they returned to the boat, Fred was drunk again, the bottle was only half full.

"Somebody coulda walked past 'im with the guns . . ."

Fred heard him. "F'one goddam dollar I'd dump them guns in the river! They the cause of all our trouble!"

"Shut up about the guns," Clete told him.

"Who you tellin' to shut up?"

"You get to drinkin', you got a big mouth," Clete said.

Fred lunged at him but Clete easily pushed him away. Then Fred clambered to the dock and staggered off, talking to himself.

Alvy said, "We shouldn't let him go like that."

"Then you go get him."

Alvy climbed out and hurried after Fred. "Fred, dammit, come on back."

"Go to hell. . . ." Fred lurched into a saloon and pushed

through a crowd of men to the bar. One of them swore and threw a punch at Fred, calling him a drunken sonofabitch.

Fred turned, with a pistol in his hand. He pulled back the hammer and two slugs hit him full in the chest, knocking him back against the bar. He dropped the gun and fell face-down in the sawdust.

Alvy stared, frozen in the spot. It was obvious that Fred was dead. The man who'd shot him walked to the body and nudged it with a boot toe. Then he holstered the pistol. He looked around at his friends. "Youall seen him draw on me."

Alvy turned and walked out to the street. There was nothing he could do for Fred now. God! It had happened in the wink of an eye. One second Fred was there—and the next—!

He stumbled back to the boat. Clete looked at him curiously. "What's the matter?"

"Fred just got hisself shot in a saloon."

Clete frowned. "You mean dead?"

Alvy nodded.

"Oh Jesus!"

Chapter Ten

LAREDO and Pete rode into Hopkins at midday. It was a sprawling town with farms on the outskirts and cattle running on the prairies. Huts and shacks were flung down along the road for miles before the town came in sight.

The main streets were dirt, rutted and muddy from a recent shower. There was a short section of street that had been cobbled in years past; it faced the largest hotel and saloon with a bank across the street. They rode past to the river and gazed at the hundred or so canoes, boats, and steamcraft moored there.

Which one was carrying Gatlings?

Laredo saw no one who looked like Alvy. "Better report," he said, and they went back to find a telegraph office. He sent a long wire to John Fleming reporting in code what had occurred since his last report, and requesting any news that Fleming might have.

The telegrapher assured them the message would go through in an hour or two. They might have an answer by the end of the day . . . or sooner with luck. "If the wire isn't down anywhere."

They dawdled in a saloon, drinking beer, eating . . . and went back to the telegraph office after several hours. A message had just come in for them. John Fleming was glad to tell them that Captain Franz Slocum of the Hopkins police was a friend, a man who had worked in Washington, D.C., for several years: "Go see him."

Fleming thanked them for the report, saying that his superior was talking to the newspapers and would probably cause them troubles thereby: "So be warned."

Fleming was an outspoken man, Laredo thought, studying the wire. He put a match to it and they went outside to find the police station.

It was a large stone building on a secondary street. They asked for Slocum and were taken to an upstairs office immediately.

Slocum was a big, portly man with steel-rimmed glasses and a leathery handshake. "John Fleming!" He became expansive. "Sit down, sit down! Salt of the earth, John Fleming. Does he still smoke those damned smelly cigars?"

"He still does," Laredo admitted.

"I dunno how his wife stands it. Whole goddam house smells of tobacco. I sometimes wonder if she smokes too."

"I'd think she'd have to."

Slocum laughed. He leaned forward over the desk, grasping his big hands. "Well, what can I do for you?"

Laredo told him about the robbery and what they'd done to date. Slocum listened, asking a question now and then. "So you think they've come here, to Hopkins?"

"It's a good guess."

"Hmmm." Slocum leaned back in his chair and stared out the near window, a finger drumming on his heavy chin. Then he turned back to them. "I think the way I can help you best is to introduce you to Lew Tolliver. Lew is pretty much our expert on the river and river traffic. He's got sources I don't know about—or want to know." He rose ponderously. "Let me get him." He went out.

"Now we're getting somewhere," Pete said.

Slocum came back with a thin wiry-looking man who gave them tight smiles and sat by the captain's desk, hands folded.

Slocum introduced them quickly and gave Tolliver a run-down on what was wanted.

Tolliver nodded, asked a few questions and said he'd read about the case in the newspapers. "You know what one of the men looks like but not the others?"

"Yes. Alvy."

"You don't know what kind of boat they have—if they have a boat?"

"Yes." Laredo felt a bit foolish. "We know very little and we guess a lot."

Tolliver smiled. "So do we. And sometimes it pays off." He examined his fingernails. "Six heavy crates, you say. Let's assume for the time being that they're all together and haven't been split up. They'd take up a little space . . ."

Pete said, "And they'd probably be guarded all the time."

"That's a good point," Tolliver agreed. "So if we're looking for a boat, it'd be one where someone is aboard day and night."

"There's another point," Laredo said. "They're killers."

"I'll keep it in mind." Tolliver nodded.

Captain Slocum said, "What about your—what shall we call them—?"

"Sources," Tolliver supplied. "Yes, I was coming to them. I have one person in mind who might know more than any other."

"Can we meet him?" Laredo asked.

"I'll ask him how he feels about it. Ordinarily I'd say no. But you're strangers, passing through . . . he might agree." Tolliver rose. "Give me a few hours." He nodded to them all and hurried out.

"He'll turn up something," Slocum assured them. "He's a very good man."

They gave Slocum the name of the hotel, the Columbia, where they could be reached, and that evening Lew Tolliver sent a message to them that he would come to the hotel at nine o'clock.

66

He was prompt, dressed in old clothes, wearing a pistol under his coat. "Hinch will meet you," he said, "on his terms. I'll have to take you a mile or so up the river. Can you pay him something?"

"What do we expect from him?" Laredo asked.

"He'll snoop along the river for us, listening at all the cracks for any word of Gatlings. It's something that none of us can do."

Laredo handed Tolliver a gold piece. "Will that cover it for now?"

"I expect so."

They saddled the horses in the stable and met Tolliver in the street. He led them out of town to the north. It was a cold night; the stars were brilliant, without a moon, and when they left the houses of the town behind it seemed colder.

Tolliver led them onto a river road and paused now and then to watch their backtrail. "I don't know why anyone would follow us, but you can't be too careful."

No one was behind them. After an hour's ride, Tolliver turned into a grove of trees and got down. He walked toward the river and whistled. Someone returned the whistle and Tolliver motioned to them to come.

Hinch lived in a kind of houseboat that looked like a converted barge. They followed Tolliver across a plank onto the deck, then down into a large cabin that smelled of cooked food. Hinch was a skinny little man, older than they had thought, and seemed happy to see Tolliver.

"Jest moved the boat over from t'other side . . ." He looked them over keenly, indicating boxes to sit on. "Who you lookin' for?"

"Man named Alvy, another named Clete. They'll prob'ly be with a third man, and we think they're on a boat and just came down river."

"What they done?"

"Stole some crates with guns in 'em."

"Ahh. Gunrunners?"

"No, we don't think so. We think they stole the guns for somebody."

Hinch looked at them slyly. "These here guns, they must be worth somethin', that right?"

"That's right," Laredo said. "They're Gatlings." He had decided they would have to tell the man about them in case he heard the word—Gatlings!

The little man's eyes widened. "How many of them?"

"Three, in packing cases, with ammunition."

"Jesiz!"

Tolliver said, "We want you to find out where they are or where the men are—or anything at all you can discover." He handed over the gold piece.

"Alvy—and Clete. Anything special about them?"

"They've killed several men recently," Tolliver said. "They don't hesitate, so don't give them any chance at you."

Hinch nodded absently. "I'll move m'boat closer to the town in the morning."

Tolliver asked, "Where'll we meet?"

"I'll come to Frenchie's late, maybe midnight."

"All right." Tolliver rose. "See you there."

Huey Getts was a lanky, rawboned man, clean-shaven, with a lantern jaw. He had been a cowhand and a gambler and for a time had run a land office until the law began to notice him.

But before that occurred he had amassed a pile of money and had begun to look around for ways to increase it quickly. The Gatling-guns situation seemed likely when he had learned about it. He could pay Clete and the others a few hundred and sell the guns for thousands. He was sure he knew exactly who he could sell them to. All he had to do was get them there.

But when he finally got free of the law and arrived at Grannie's place he was disappointed. The men and the guns

68

were gone. He shouted at old Grannie, "Why the hell did you let them go?"

Grannie was miffed. "How could I stop 'em? They was three to my one!"

"You mean four . . ."

"No. Ira got hisself shot."

"Who shot him?"

Grannie shrugged. "Think it was bounty hunters. Maybe Rangers."

"Shit!" Getts paced the room. "Izzat why they went, to dodge the law?"

"No, because they was broke. Didn't have no cash at all. Hell, they owe me seventeen dollars!"

Getts kicked the wall.

Grannie said, "You want to gi' me the seventeen?"

"Why should I? It's not my bill to pay. Where did they go?"

"Downriver is all I know." Grannie made a face and shrugged. "They didn't tell me nothing."

Getts swore and stormed out. He went into Humboldt, looking for a boat.

Grannie watched him go and smiled evilly. The cheap sonofabitch. To hell with Getts. He had not told Getts about the letter Clete was going to leave him in Hopkins.

Getts ought to have more respect for his elders.

No one wanted to hire out for a trip downriver. Getts went from one boat owner to the next. Finally he came across a barge owner who was going downstream and agreed to take him for a price.

"How far you goin'?"

Getts frowned. Where the hell *was* he going? "The next big town."

The barge man nodded. "That'll be Hopkins. Take you for two dollars."

Getts paid it over, and as the barge slowly swung out into the current he knew he was on a fool's errand. There were

69

hundreds of towns downriver and the three men with the crates could be in any one of them.

And he knew none of them by sight.

Chapter Eleven

HINCH had never been a man of schedule or even of his word. He was a willow in the wind, doing what he could get away with, always on the shady side of the law, with loyalty only to himself.

He drank up the gold coin that Lew Tolliver had given him, and lay drunk for a day in his bargeboat, adding to its smells.

And when sobriety finally came his way, he was broke and hungry. But he knew he could not go back to Tolliver for more monetary help. He set out to beg in the town.

This was successful and he garnered enough to buy himself a good meal and another bottle. But when he began to tip it up it occurred to him that a future without Lew Tolliver might be arduous. Perhaps it would be better to do a little work.

He began to wander along the waterfront, chatting here and there, telling a few lies, listening for the right words.

When he met Tolliver that night near midnight, he had little to report on the subject of Gatlings. So far there was not even a rumor. He had found a half dozen people living aboard boats but it was not a sensible idea to ask them their names. People were touchy.

"Keep at it," Tolliver said.

"Who were those men you brought to my boat, Laredo and the Mexican?"

"Government men. They work for a government agency."

"They're lawmen like you?"

"Investigators. They report to Washington, D.C. What do you care?"

"Just curious, Mr. Tolliver. That's all."

He kept at it and the next day noticed two men who were apparently living aboard a boat named *Rondo*. He paid attention to them because they seemed furtive—small indications gave him that notion. And then he heard one of them call the other "Clete."

Hinch smiled to himself. So the Gatlings were aboard that boat. And they were valuable?

He went into a saloon and sat by himself in a corner, thinking it over. He would have to tell Lew Tolliver that he had seen the men or that he had not. Would Tolliver believe him if he said he had failed? Maybe and maybe not. If he thought he was being lied to, then Tolliver would cut him loose. It was a serious question because often Tolliver had been the difference between eating and going hungry. No, he didn't want to lose the money that Tolliver gave him.

But Tolliver didn't have to know if he made a deal with Kyle Dengler. Who would tell him? Dengler would pay him a good deal of money to know about the Gatlings. Hinch was certain of it.

Now he had to find Dengler.

And he knew it would not prove to be easy. Kyle Dengler was the biggest dealing-man in town, maybe in the entire area. He dealt in everything that would turn a dollar—no matter who it belonged to. He had an organization that, it was rumored, would even permanently dispose of someone for the right price. Kyle Dengler was vicious and unscrupulous—but he had money. He could pay for information.

Hinch went to every saloon in town, leaving word with bartenders that he had something to say to Dengler.

And the next night, very late, Dengler came to see him at the houseboat barge. Hinch had just returned from the hotel where he had talked to Tolliver, saying he still hadn't heard a whisper about the Gatlings.

Dengler was a big man who moved like a cat. He showed up with two others who looked inside, then kept watch at the door. Dengler came inside as if he owned the barge and sat down opposite an astonished and frightened Hinch.

In a deceptively soft voice Dengler asked, "You wanted to see me?"

Hinch did his best to smile, hoping Dengler would not notice his trembling. "I—I got something to s-sell."

"Tell me."

"It a-ain't going no farther?"

Dengler looked pained. "Of course not. What is it?"

"Information."

"Go on."

"I know where something is. Easy to get at and worth a lot."

"You have to tell me more than that."

Hinch took a breath. He was in too deep now. There was no way he could back out. He said, "Gatling guns." He saw the surprise in the other.

Dengler pursed his lips. "You mean the guns been in the newspapers?"

"The same ones. I know where they are."

Dengler stared at him silently. "How do you happen to know all this?"

Hinch took a long chance. "I got drunk with one of them an' he talked too much."

"You know him?"

Hinch nodded. "From a long time back." He thought Dengler swallowed the story. Wasn't it plausible?

"All right. Where are they?"

"Let's talk about money first."

73

Dengler smiled. "You ought to trust me more, little man. I don't have to pay you anything if I don't want to."

Hinch wailed, "Ever'body says you's a fair man!"

"That's right. Where are the guns?"

"How much do—"

Dengler moved closer. "You've already said too much, Hinch. I could squeeze it all out of you. Izzat what you want?"

"No, no, no."

"Tell me where the guns are."

Hinch sighed deeply. "They're on a boat named *Rondo*. It's right on the waterfront."

"How many on board?"

"They 'sposed to be three, but I only seen two."

Dengler nodded. He rose and counted out a wad of bills, dropping them on a box. "Thanks, little friend." He went out quickly.

Hinch counted the money. Two hundred dollars. It was more than he'd ever expected! He put most of it away in a secret place. The next morning he went out and bought himself a bottle of good whiskey.

There was no way he could tell how fast Kyle Dengler might move to acquire the guns, but Hinch thought he'd wait till the next night. Men like Dengler were partial to nightfall.

He had a long pull at the bottle, then wrote a short note to Lew Tolliver: "Guns on boat *Rondo*." He paid a young boy a half-dime to deliver the note to the police station. He watched the boy go in, then he hurried to his barge home and stayed there. He had done his best for Mr. Tolliver, hadn't he?

Hinch had no idea how fast Dengler could move.

Dengler had gone to see Hinch near midnight and in two hours he and his men had located the boat *Rondo*. It was a wide-bottomed scow, battered and dirty. There was no light on board and no one in evidence.

74

The waterfront was quiet and dark. Dengler and two men stood in the shadows, peering at the boat. Dengler said, "We'll cut it loose and push if off into the river . . . nice and easy."

Handy asked, "What about them on board?"

"You and Bert slip down into the cabin and fix 'em."

"It'll be darker'n hell, K.," Bert protested.

Dengler nodded. "All right. Handy scratches a match and you fix 'em both. Can you do that? They'll prob'ly be asleep."

Bert nodded. "All right."

"Then we'll drop down the river a couple miles. Let's get moving." Dengler led the way to the boat.

Handy cut the bowline and Bert slipped the sternline quickly. Dengler was already on board, the tiller in his hand. The two pushed off gently and the scow moved sluggishly into the current.

Dengler pointed to the long pole lying in the bottom of the boat. Handy took it and poled them strongly. In minutes they were away from the docks, quiet as a ripple, moving onto the misty river.

Then Bert and Handy went below, silent as Indians in the dark. Dengler saw the instant glow as a match was scratched. He smiled.

In a few moments Handy came on deck. "They was only two of them."

Dengler shrugged. "Are the crates down there?"

Handy nodded. "You want we should toss them two over?"

"Hell no. We'll bury them on shore soon's it gets light. I want them to disappear without a trace."

Lew Tolliver reported to Captain Slocum, giving him Hinch's note. Slocum sent a man to the hotel to notify Laredo and Torres that he was organizing a raiding party and the two met Slocum at the waterfront.

"It's not here," Pete said, after a look.

The boat *Rondo* had gone in the night. Slocum's men could find no one who had seen it go.

The captain returned to the station to wire law officers downstream to be on the lookout for the *Rondo*. Lew Tolliver hurried to call on Hinch.

He found Hinch drunk, sprawled on his bunk bed, the bottle half empty. Hinch was snoring.

Tolliver poured water on him and Hinch sat up sputtering, swearing. "Wha-th-hell—" He bleared at Tolliver and finally recognized him. "Wha' you wan'?"

"You little sonofabitch, you sold us out, didn't you?"

"What?"

"The boat's gone." Tolliver picked up the whiskey bottle, pointing to the label. "You sold us out . . . izzat how you're buying expensive whiskey?"

"You g-gimme a gold p-piece."

Tolliver scowled. That's right, they had.

Hinch blinked at him. "The boat's gone?"

"You told them we were going to raid, didn't you?"

"I did not!" Hinch was affronted. "I tole 'em nothing!" He almost sputtered in his righteousness. "I never went near 'at boat!"

Tolliver sat down on a box and stared at the little crook. Was it possible the whole thing was a coincidence? The men on the boat had decided to move, hours before the police raid? He didn't care much for coincidences—but they *did* happen. And he didn't really believe Hinch—but deep down he was sure Hinch was telling the truth this time. He hadn't gone near the boat.

"I would'n do sich a thing," Hinch said, shaking his head.

Tolliver sighed and got up.

He reported to Captain Slocum his opinion that Hinch had not informed those on the boat that they were about to be raided.

"I don't like the way it happened," Slocum said. "Everything points to this 'source.' "

"He hasn't got the guts of a toad, and drunk as he was, I think he was surprised when I told him the boat was gone."

"Damn! Well, I'll have to inform Garrett and Torres and let them go on from here. You think the boat's gone downstream?"

"Probably. Unless they crossed to the other side. I'll get men on that angle."

"Yes, good."

Laredo and Pete Torres were very unhappy at the news. Lew Tolliver told them himself, and told them his reasons for believing Hinch had not betrayed them.

But when Tolliver had gone, Laredo said, "What's the odds that Hinch told somebody else—not the men on the boat?"

Pete nodded. "That would do it. Who would he tell, someone to raid the boat?"

"It's another guess. Would Hinch know someone like that?"

"He's a crook," Pete said. "He'd know *about* someone like that. He'd know how to get word to him."

"Yes, he would. I think you've hit it."

"But how much help is it? Where the hell is the boat?"

Laredo frowned. "Another guess. Downstream is the quickest way out of here."

"They could go across the river . . ."

"If they did, how about the crates? They'd have to get a wagon in the middle of the night—then get rid of the boat."

"Yeh." Pete smiled. "They went downstream."

In less than half an hour they were saddling the horses in the stable. There was a river road and they took it, hurrying southeast. The road did not follow each undulation of the river, moving a mile or more away from it now and then and running close by other times.

On one of these Laredo halted. "How far have we come, five, six miles?"

"Probably."

"How far would they come at night—if they had raided the boat, I mean."

Pete said, "I don't follow you."

"If someone in the town had raided the boat, how far would they come? Wouldn't they have to go back for a wagon?" He stared at the river. "They would know that Captain Slocum would wire downstream and set up blocks . . . wouldn't they?"

"I'd think so. You mean we've come too far?"

"Maybe."

"You mean something else too. You think Clete and the others are dead."

Laredo nodded. "I'm afraid so. Why would they leave anyone alive? And they'd have to get off the river."

"So somebody walked into town for a wagon."

"That's the way I see it. I suggest we talk to Slocum and get him to organize a search."

"For the boat."

"Yes. If we can find the boat . . ." Laredo shrugged. "We may find something else."

Chapter Twelve

CAPTAIN Slocum was surprised to see them. "Lew told me you'd cleared out this morning."

"We've got a theory," Laredo said. "If someone raided the boat late at night and took it downstream, they wouldn't go far."

"Why not?"

"They'd know you would wire ahead. We think they put the crates on a wagon and started west with them. If we can find the boat—"

"I get you." Slocum got up. "I'll get men on it right now." He paused at the door. "I want you to go along to identify them."

"We will."

As they went down to the horses, Pete said, "He thinks they're dead too."

Slocum appointed Lew Tolliver to be in charge of the search party. He divided them into two groups of five men each and they rode following the river. Five men galloped ahead and began to work their way back.

In two hours they found the boat.

It had been pulled into a tiny inlet and covered with cut brush so it was entirely hidden from the river side.

Below, in the cabin, there was blood on the bunks and the

deck. "They were knifed," Tolliver said. "Probably in their sleep."

On shore were the tracks of a wagon. They led out to the river road and blended with hundreds of others.

Laredo asked, "Where are the bodies?"

Tolliver motioned to the men. "Spread out and find the graves. They probably buried them."

It took an hour. One of the men finally noticed fresh earth under a blanket of dry leaves and when the leaves were scraped away, two low mounds were seen.

"Dig 'em out," Tolliver ordered.

The bodies had been rolled in blankets. One of them was Alvy. Laredo recognized it immediately, but not the other.

Pete said, "Why only two? There were three."

There was no answer.

But there was a big question: Who now had the guns? This was obviously murder and robbery, as Tolliver said. Someone got wind of the guns and had acquired them.

Tolliver ordered the men reburied a little deeper, and they returned to the city. He said, "I'll see what I can find out about who is missing from his usual haunts. That won't tell us where he is, but it'll tell us *who* he is."

That would probably take a few days.

Laredo said, "By then the trail will be cold. What if Pete and I go on, see what we can turn up, and we'll wire you in a week or so?"

"Good idea," Tolliver agreed.

They stayed the night at the Columbia and left early in the morning. There was not much travel on the river road—most used the river—but there had been travel on it for decades and it was rutted and often stony, and often a hundred feet wide.

They watched for a wheeled vehicle that turned off the road. The guns would make deep wheel marks in the earth that might be very difficult to brush away.

There were few roads or paths that turned off till they

reached the next town. It was a sleepy little burg named Dolat—after its oldest resident, they were told. After some questioning they learned that a wagon had come through the town, with strangers on it . . . three men. They had stopped at the general store to buy necessities and had told the storekeeper they were farmers returning home after a trip upriver.

The storekeeper thought that one of them had been named Bert. The man who had paid was a big man. "Big as you," he said to Pete. "And I tell you, he wasn't no farmer. Had hands like a gambler."

"Did they say where they were bound?"

The storekeeper shook his head.

One of the men sitting in a tilted-back chair facing the street told them the wagon had taken the road west out of town. "Didn't foller the river," he said.

"Where's that road go?"

"Goes to Lynchville, thirty mile or so. They's a telegraph there."

"But not one here?"

"No."

It was rolling prairie outside of town, probably all the way to the Rockies. The tracks of the heavily laden wagon were fresh on the earth; the murderers were not many hours ahead of them—whoever they were.

But an hour outside of Dolat it began to drizzle and in a short time the rain came down. Laredo and Torres shrugged into slickers and went on, heads down, not stopping to eat when it got dark.

The road became a muddy track, but easy to see in the gloom, and they came to Lynchville hours after dark; the town was closed up, not even a saloon open. It was a slightly larger place than little Dolat, with a few dozen structures that could be called houses, amid half a hundred shacks and sheds, even some tents.

They rode through the town, looking at every building, but

81

it was impossible to tell if the wagon was housed there. The tracks had long since disappeared. Had they gone on or not?

The livery stable on the main street was locked up tight but there was a corral and a large shed next to it. The shed contained several bales of hay and nothing else, and the door had no latch. They pulled the saddles off the horses, put them in the corral and bedded down in the shed. At least it was dry.

It rained all night long, not hard, but steady, and eased up in the morning. When the livery opened, the owner charged them two bits for the lodging and another two bits for horse fodder. They went across the street to a restaurant, and from there to the telegraph office.

The telegrapher was a middle-age man with a large stomach and steel-rimmed glasses which he looked over at them. Laredo asked if a large man, a stranger, had sent a message the night or day before.

"I can't tell you that. Rules."

Laredo showed his credentials and the man was impressed. "Government man, huh?"

"We're after some murderers."

"There was a man in here, large fella. Sent a wire to Fowler. That's down south of here, three, four hundred miles." The telegrapher fiddled in a box and brought out a yellow sheet. "Addressed to a T. R. Rollins. The wire says: 'Meet me at Bucklin.' It's signed: Dengler."

"What's Bucklin?"

"Got no idea. Could be any one of a thousand small towns. Could be somebody's name."

"Dengler," Pete Torres said. "That's his name, huh. No initial?"

"That's it. Dengler."

Laredo jotted down the names. "Thanks."

"Hope you catch 'em."

"You got a map of the area that shows Fowler?"

The telegrapher pointed. "One on the wall there."

Lynchville, the town they were in, was circled heavily with a lead pencil. Two main roads led out of the town, one running east and west, the other slanting from northeast to southwest, generally. None of the roads traveled a straight line. Some followed Indian trails laid down centuries past.

It took them a few minutes to locate Fowler. As the telegrapher had said, it was south, about four hundred miles as Laredo marked it off. There were several ways to get there, none direct.

Pete squinted at the map. "Don't see a Bucklin anywhere."

Laredo agreed. "Me neither." Of course a lot of tiny burgs were not on any map and not likely to be. Some towns didn't last long; if a mine played out, the town vanished. Some burned down and went up again somewhere else. There was lots of land. Towns often withered and died if they weren't on a crossroads or next to an army post or at some convenient place.

Laredo sent a telegram to John Fleming, reporting their movements: "Now heading for Fowler, will wire from there."

He also wired Captain Slocum as promised, telling him about T. R. Rollins and the man Dengler. Dengler had two men with him. One of the three was named Bert.

The message to Slocum had to be routed several hundred miles to Hopkins—there was no direct wire—and the line was down somewhere along the way. It would be repaired in several hours, the telegrapher told them, but they did not wait for an answer.

They bought airtights at the store, a few other necessities, and were on their way inside an hour. It did not rain and in several hours the road dried, a pleasant change.

The wagon tracks had long ago been obliterated, but in the first small town they came to, a few remembered a wagon and three men.

"You ever hear of a place called Bucklin?" Pete asked a storekeeper.

"Never did," The man replied.

The next settlement they came to was not big enough to be called a town. It was a collection of five shacky buildings, one a saloon and one a trading post. It was on the edge of a wide dry wash on a bit of high ground, treeless and bare.

The sign on the saloon, scrubbed on in axle grease, read: GREELY.

They tied the horses in front and went inside; the room was empty except for a man writing on a sheet of foolscap at the end of the bar. He looked up. "Howdy, gents."

"Howdy," Laredo said. "You Mr. Greely?"

"Nope. They was a Greely here five, six years ago but he died of something or other. You lookin' to see him?"

"No. Saw the sign outside."

"Ahh. I ain't bothered to change it. Bought the place from his widow. She went east some'eres."

Laredo asked about Dengler and the wagon, but the man shook his head. "Ain't been anybody through here in a week . . . comin' from north, that is. Had a big party through here four days ago, but they was one of them travelin' troupes, pokin' up north."

When they were alone, Pete said, "Dengler turned off. He headed across the prairie."

"Which way?"

"We got to go and find out."

They backtracked, watching for wheel marks that turned off the road and found none.

Halfway back to Lynchville, Pete said, "They picked up the goddam wagon and carried it out into the prairie."

'The horses, too?"

"If they can pick up the wagon they can pick up the horses."

Laredo grinned. An interesting picture. He said, "I think we've underestimated Mr. Dengler."

"In what way?"

"He knows he's being followed—or suspects it."

"Then why did he send that telegram?"

"What did we learn from it? If we knew about Bucklin, I'd agree with you, but it could be anything—a man, a place—"

"We should have asked Fleming about Dengler. He may have a record."

Laredo shrugged. "Would Fleming know about it?"

"We could ask."

"All right." Laredo looked at the sky. "We'd better go on to Lynchville. It'll be dark by the time we get there. I'm beginning to think you're right about picking up the wagon."

They had steaks in a restaurant in Lynchville and sent another wire to Fleming asking about Dengler. They stayed in the only hotel, a drafty structure with lumpy beds and no sheets. In the morning they had a reply from Fleming. A man named Kyle Dengler was wanted for murder in several states; he had last been seen in Kansas City. He was considered very dangerous.

When they left the town, Laredo suggested they part, each moving off the road a hundred yards to look for wagon tracks. They did this and found the tracks immediately . . . pointing west.

"A slippery sonofabitch!" Pete said. "He turned off the road two seconds after he left the town! And we went all the way to Greely and back!"

"We've underestimated this one. We got careless."

Chapter Thirteen

Bᴇʀᴛ was unhappy about leaving Hopkins, where he had a girl. It had been a spur-of-the-moment thing and he'd had no time to tell her anything.

"There's girls everywhere," Dengler said. "You can get yourself a half dozen when we sell the Gatlings."

"I want this girl. I'd want none of them others."

"You're sure particular . . ."

"How long're we going to be gone?"

"How the hell can I tell that," Dengler said with exasperation. "As long as it takes."

They had turned off the road just outside of Lynchville and brushed out the tracks for a short distance. Dengler was sure the police would find the boat *Rondo* eventually; and someone was undoubtedly actively seeking the stolen guns . . . so sooner or later they would be followed. He had to figure that way. The police were not stupid. They would ask a hell of a lot of questions and someone was bound to remember something . . . though he was positive no one had seen them steal the boat.

His plan was simple. He would meet Rollins at the Bucklin stage stop and they would negotiate a sale.

All he had to do was get there.

They went straight across the prairie, bending left after several hours. Dengler had a compass and consulted it several times a day. He was making for Evanstown on the railroad. On this course they should cut the railroad in another day, then follow the rails into the town.

From Evanstown they would take a trader's road south.

That night Bert groused more. Every mile was taking him away from the girl and he worried that she had no word from him at all. Handy laughed at him and Dengler refused to talk about it.

Privately Dengler hoped he would build up a head of steam over the distant girl and go back to her. And lose his share. Bert was no longer needed by them.

Dengler's navigation was good enough to get them to the railroad tracks. They stretched away in both directions, silent and unresponsive. His navigation was not good enough to tell him which way they should go to find Evanstown. He had a hunch it was to the west. And after some discussion they went that way.

It proved to be the right way. In another day they saw the lights of the town in the distance as night fell.

Evanstown was not much. It was a waterstop and little else. A stageline connected and there was a street of eleven stores and saloons. South and west was cattle country and on weekends there were always cowhands in town, shooting at the stars and spending what money they had.

They put up at the only hotel. It was as poor as Dengler had ever seen, with built-in bunks and no locks on the doors. Inside the rooms were short pieces of wood nailed next to the door; the wooden slats could be turned to hold the door closed. The building had been painted inside when built and not since, the outside had once been whitewashed. Dengler collected his warbag and rifle and went upstairs to a room, tired to death.

Handy did the same, but Bert went into the saloon for a drink. It was a weekday night and few were around; the bartender was engrossed in a newspaper. Bert sipped the whiskey and looked out the front window at the station building across the way.

There was a sign: TELEGRAPH OFFICE.

Finishing the drink, he got up and hurried out. He would send her a wire and Dengler would never know.

Captain Slocum showed the wire from Laredo to Lew Tolliver. Kyle Dengler was their man, and Tolliver reported that Dengler had suddenly disappeared from his usual haunts and had not been seen for days. Tolliver's sources told him that a man nicknamed Handy was no longer in evidence either.

How had Dengler gotten into the affair? Very suspicious, Tolliver called on Hinch and found the little man recovering from a bout of drunkenness, feeling sorry for himself and somehow very frightened when he saw Tolliver. Mentioning jail in his initial conversation, Tolliver leaned heavily on Hinch. "What do you know about Kyle Dengler?"

"D-Dengler? I don't know 'im!"

"I think you do."

Hinch was visibly shaking. "What w-would he do wi' the likes of me?"

"You've heard about him?"

Hinch nodded. He could admit that.

"Who are his friends?"

"I d-don't know."

"Find out." Tolliver got up. "I'll be back tomorrow."

Hinch knew there was no way out for him. He would have to tell Tolliver . . . and hope he would believe it was information just turned up. But then, why should he not believe it?

He seemed to, when Hinch told him. "Dengler's seen wi' two, Handy and Bert Penry."

"Where do they hang out?"

Hinch shook his head. "I don't know."

Tolliver went away. He reported what he'd learned to Captain Slocum.

Two days later, while Slocum was sifting through the telegraph copies that were supplied him each morning, he came across one signed: Bert. It had been sent from a place called Evanstown.

It said that he was with D and they were on a business trip and would be back in a week or two.

It was sent to a woman named Sarah Longtree.

Lew Tolliver went to see her at the address given. It was a dingy hotel next to a saloon. Sarah was a dancehall girl who slept until noon each day. When he rapped on her door he could hear voices inside, a woman's and a man's. But when she opened the door the man had gone. Possibly out the window, Tolliver thought. He did not ask her about it.

He did ask her about Bert.

"Yeah, I know a Bert." She gazed at him curiously. "What's he done?"

"We think he killed two men."

"Eee," she made a noise in her throat. "It'd be like 'im. You mean in a fight?"

"No. I mean murder." He watched her eyes dilate. Sarah was not pretty; she was not a day under forty, he was sure, and her eyes never met his for more than an instant.

He asked, "Where is he now?"

"I dunno. I haven't seen him for a while."

"You got a telegram from him."

"Oh. You know about that?"

"Yes. We have a copy. Who is D?"

She sighed. "Dengler, I guess. Bert hung out with him. Who'd he kill?"

Tolliver shook his head. "Do you know a man called Handy?"

She nodded. "He hung out with Dengler too."

"Have you had Handy up here?"

She stared at him brazenly for a moment. "Sure. I ain't married to nobody."

He went to the door, glanced back at her and went out.

"She works in a dancehall," he reported to Slocum. "She knows Bert and Handy and probably Dengler. Can you get word to Garrett and Torres?"

"I'll wire the sheriff of that county to take the bunch into custody. Don't know how to reach the two—but they must be following Dengler."

"Probably."

They lost the wagon tracks in the prairie sod and could not pick them up again. The wind was against them, and a light rain did not help.

When they reached a railroad track they turned east following a long curve and came to a town that sprawled on both sides of the tracks. There were extensive loading chutes and corrals and the place smelled of cows. It was called Crowley and, being on the railroad, had a telegraph.

Laredo wired John Fleming to report where they were. Then he wired Captain Slocum and had an answer within the hour. Kyle Dengler was their man, and the two with him were undoubtedly Handy and Bert Penry . . . both very dangerous characters. Bert had wired a girl from Evanstown three days ago.

Slocum could tell them nothing about T.R. Rollins.

Evanstown, the station master told them, was fifty miles west. "You can cut off about seven miles by going straight across." He pointed.

Pete asked, "Is there a train going that way?"

"Yep. In four days."

They rode across country, navigating a small section of badlands and arrived in Evanstown the next day. Dengler, the wagon and two others had been there and gone south. The county sheriff had also been there, looking for Dengler, the saloon-keeper told them.

"Slocum wired him," Laredo said to Pete. "What you think?"

"I agree. But I don't think Dengler knows we're on his trail. We haven't been near him yet."

The station master supplied them with a map, the best he had. This country hadn't been surveyed, he told them, except for the railroad right-of-way, so nothing on the map was particularly accurate. "Lot of guesswork goes into it. Folks measure distances by painting a line on a wagon wheel and counting the turns—but sometimes they mess up the counts."

An old trading route led south from Evanstown, the road Dengler had taken. But there were numerous crossroads farther south and he could have taken any of them. Fowler was still two hundred miles away.

In Hopkins, Huey Getts haunted the saloons and spread money around, asking for news, gossip or information about Clete and the boat *Rondo*.

He heard a lot of stories, most farfetched, made up out of whole cloth. He knew enough to make a stab at sorting truth from wild fiction. And sooner or later he came to Hinch.

He was not much impressed by the little man at first, but when Hinch mentioned Alvy and Fred, Getts knew he was on the right track. They had met in a saloon, but he got Hinch to take him to the barge houseboat where they would not be overheard, and he laid a gold piece in Hinch's eager hand.

"Tell me what you know about the *Rondo*."

Before Getts left, Hinch had collected three gold pieces.

He stayed drunk for almost three weeks.

Chapter Fourteen

KYLE Dengler felt very secure, leaving Evanstown behind. There had been no pursuit, because he was certain they had left nothing but a very faint trail. Good trackers were few and far between; certainly the average lawman had few of those skills.

His only annoyance was Bert Penry. Bert was whining and grousing more and more. What in hell did that girl have that made him so unhappy to be away from her?

Handy told him he had bedded the girl and there was nothing special about her. Maybe she was the only female who had ever said a kind word to Bert. Dengler agreed that was probably it. When he suggested that Bert could leave them at any time and go back to her, Bert only glared at him.

But the suggestion seemed to work inside of Bert like a cancer. When they camped the second night he brought it to a head. "You tryin' to get rid of me?"

Dengler said, "For crissakes, Bert, all you doing is making trouble. You want t'go back to that goddam girl, you go ahead. We'll send you your share."

Bert did not believe that for a minute, and his face showed it. He looked at Handy, who laughed.

Dengler slipped a derringer into his hand. Bert was seething and there was no telling what he might do. He was thinking of a way to cool the situation when Handy told Bert he was a fool to worry about one girl.

Bert said, "She's a damn good woman."

"Yeh," Handy said, "I know." He laughed. "I been in her bed too."

Bert went for his gun, screaming with rage. It cleared his holster when Dengler shot him twice with the over-and-under .41. Bert stared at him with round eyes and fell to his knees. The pistol dropped from lifeless fingers and Bert sprawled in the dirt.

Handy was astonished. "The sombitch woulda shot me!"

"What the hell did you figure? You was goading him."

Handy turned the body over. "He's dead as hell, D. You centered him. Now what d'we do?"

Dengler stood up and gazed around. It was getting dark and they were alone, miles from anyone. He reloaded the little gun and put it away. "We bury him. What else?"

They dug a hole a hundred yards off the trail, wrapped the body in a blanket and laid it on the bottom. Handy said, "He ain't never going to see that gal now. Poor sonofabitch."

They filled in the dirt, tramped it down and moved down the road a mile or two.

In the morning they went on.

Sheriff Bodie Ankers had missed Dengler and the others at Evanstown—after the wire from Slocum. The wagon had gone south, so he immediately wired ahead to Pearson, giving the deputy there the description of Dengler and the two with him.

He neglected to include in the wire any information about the crates in the wagon, assuming that the wagon would be impounded and its contents noted.

His deputy at Pearson was a brave and honest young man but not a thoughtful one. His name was Ralph Abbott and when he received instructions from Sheriff Ankers he immediately formed a posse of eight men from the town, saw that they were well-armed, and met Dengler and Handy on the road, placing them under arrest without opposition.

"What's the charge?" Dengler demanded.

" 'Cording to the Sheriff, youall shot and buried two gents."

Dengler looked at him in astonishment. "You got the wrong *hombres*, deputy. We never shot anybody!"

Handy shook his head. "Never did."

"Well, mebbe so. But I got to take you in till it gets straightened out."

The jail at Pearson was adobe, several feet thick, with a log roof overlaid with dirt on which grass was growing. They put the wagon in the stable behind the jail and the team in the corral beside it. It never occurred to Deputy Abbott to look under the tarpaulin on the wagon. He was only concerned with the two men.

He put them in two of the six small cells the town owned. After supper he wired Sheriff Ankers that the men were in custody.

He received an answer the next morning that Ankers would send two men to get them.

Deputy Ralph Abbott was the only law in Pearson, a usually sleepy, very peaceable town where almost nothing happened of a violent nature. The town had a church and a large dry-goods store and women from the entire region sent there for fripperies and dress goods. Though it was in cow country, cowhands avoided the town, giving their business instead to Brush Creek, a town ten miles west. It had no church and seven saloons.

Abbott had been instructed to make rounds several times a day and, being a serious-minded young man, he did as he was told.

It was necessary to have someone to look after the jailhouse while Abbott was on the rounds, so young Charles Bowman had been hired. Charlie was only nineteen; he sat at Abbott's battered desk and read his law books—he figured to go to law school one day. Charlie was also an orphan, living with an uncle and aunt who fought continually when the uncle, Hiram Bowman, was home.

Hiram worked as a day-laborer for several of the merchants in town. He was an ex-convict, which few knew, and had a very poor outlook on life. He had decided long since that most were against him, including his wife, and he longed to get away from Pearson, change his name, and settle somewhere else. He dreamed about it constantly. He put money aside from his wages—that his wife did not know about—for that day. He had no intention of taking her along.

When Hiram heard about the two fugitives in the town jail it aroused his curiosity and he went to look at them when Deputy Abbott was away. Hiram, a gaunt, lantern-jawed man, usually unshaven, was always interested in seeing someone more unfortunate than himself. These two in the jail would hang soon, young Charlie told him. Sheriff Ankers had wired that they were guilty as hell.

Charlie happened to mention that the prisoner's wagon was in the stable, and Hiram, going that way anyhow, went inside to look at that too.

And noticed the tarpaulin.

No one was around. Hiram leaned over the wagon tail and stared at the taut dark green tarpaulin. What was under it? He untied it and drew it back to peer at the crates. The closest one bore the legend: WOODRUFF ARSENAL US ARMY.

What the hell were these—guns? With mounting excitement, Hiram found a prybar and inserted it in a crack, lifting the top of one crate. He stared down at the strange-

95

looking metal sections and realized he was looking at Gatling guns!

"Jesus Christ!" Those men in the jail were gunrunners!

He hammered the lid down again. These guns were worth money! A lot of money—to the right buyer. And they belonged to a couple of losers who were about to hang!

He tied the tarpaulin back as he had found it and sat down to think about it. He could sell those guns in any big town—like Hanford, which was only forty miles away.

Then he'd have enough money to get out for good.

The jail routine was simple. Very few were ever incarcerated and then usually only for drunken behavior. Serious crimes were almost unknown in Pearson. When no one was being held in the jail, Deputy Abbott locked up and went home nights. But with a prisoner or two he slept on a cot in the office.

The stable was not close to the jail building, and the jail and office were of thick adobe, one long building with a log roof. It would be almost impossible for a man sleeping in the office to hear ordinary sounds from the stable.

His hardest task, Hiram thought, would be to get out of the house without his wife asking damnfool questions: "Where are you going at this hour?"

He thought about it, looking at the wagon with its tarpaulin, and decided not to go home at all that night. Even if she went looking for him she would never in the world think of looking in the jailhouse stable. He had some money saved at the house, but it was not a great amount. He shrugged it off and climbed into the stable loft and made himself comfortable. In a while he drifted off to sleep.

When it was full dark he woke and stared into the gloom, feeling hungry. Well, he could stand a little hunger when he was on the verge of making a killing. He passed the next hours thinking about how much he might get for the guns . . . then dreaming about where he would go and what he would do.

He had never been east of St. Louis; his parents had taken him there when he was seven or eight. All he recalled of it was seeing the steamboats on the river.

When he judged it was time, he climbed down from the loft and saw that most of the house lights were out. People went to bed early, depending on how many games of checkers one wanted to play.

Opening the rear door of the stable, he began to pull the wagon out. He was wiry strong and when he got the wheels turning it came rather easily, squeaking and groaning a bit, noises that seemed loud in the stillness, but he got it rolled out to the street and went back for the horses. He took down the corral poles and led the horses out one by one, making very little sound.

Hooking up the wagon, he drove away slowly. It had been easier than he'd feared.

But now the die was cast. He was now liable to arrest himself . . . he could go back to jail . . . grand theft. If they caught him. *If* they caught him.

He drove through part of the town to reach the Hanford road. He could have gone the other way, to Bannock, a slightly larger town, but he knew Hanford better. He would take the guns to old Paddy Capwell who bought and sold anything likely. Paddy always had cash. Paddy discounted everything, but he had cash. And he never asked embarrassing questions.

Hiram turned onto the road and clucked up the horses. He ought to be in Hanford by dawn.

Laredo and Torres took the road south; the next large town was Pearson, if one followed the road. The wagon could have turned off as before and gone across the prairie. To guard against this possibility their progress was slow as they scanned every yard of ground on both sides of the road looking for telltale marks.

They found a few but when they followed up on them, the tracks soon petered out.

Pete said, "I think this time they stayed on the road. They don't figure they're followed."

"I think you're right. Let's go on into Pearson."

Pete nodded.

Chapter Fifteen

THE adobe walls of the Pearson jail were thick, the single window of Dengler's cell was tiny and high up; it was too small for a man's shoulders and thus had no bars. The roof was heavy logs, each one a foot or more in diameter. No exit that way.

The only way out was through the barred door.

He and Handy discussed escape when they were alone in the cell area. They had adjoining cells. Their only possibility seemed to be in grabbing the deputy—if he came in close enough—pulling him against the bars hard enough to knock him out, then getting the keys.

Deputy Ralph Abbott was pleasant enough but wary. The first few times he brought them food, he had them back up to the rear of the cells before he slipped the trays under the bars.

Dengler swore about it considerably when the deputy had gone.

There was some sort of furor the next morning. When Deputy Abbott opened the door from the office to bring them breakfast they could hear excited voices—then Abbott closed the door. He would tell them nothing but they could see he was angry.

At noon the young man, Charlie Bowman, brought them plates of food and coffee in white mugs, staying well out of their reach. He would say nothing despite their questions. He had orders to keep his mouth shut, he told them.

Something had happened that concerned them, Dengler was sure. Else why would no one talk to them?

"Maybe they dug up them bodies by the river."

"Naw. They'll never find them. It's something else."

"They found the guns in the wagon."

Dengler shook his head. "Hell, they found them yesterday when they brought us here."

"Yeh, I guess so."

When Charlie Bowman came into the cell area to pick up the trays—their chance came. Inexperienced, Charlie got careless. He had to reach too far under the bars to get hold of Handy's tray, and Handy jumped and managed to grab him and yank him close. Dengler grabbed his head and banged it hard on one of the steel bars and the boy went limp.

"Get the keys!"

Handy tore the key ring off the boy's belt. In moments he had the cell door open, then opened Dengler's. They dragged Charlie inside and locked the cell.

In the office they found revolvers and rifles on a rack. In the corral were three horses. Dengler looked at the stable; the wagon and crates were probably there—but there was no time. A posse on horseback would run a wagon down in a hurry and they'd be back behind bars again.

In five minutes they were riding out of town, taking the road to Bannock—the first road they came to. In twenty minutes the town was behind them.

They were free!

Huey Getts left Hopkins driving a light buckboard with a single horse. He was sure that the guns would go no farther on the river. It would be too well watched.

He was sure too, that the guns had been taken over by someone else, if Hinch could be believed. Hinch thought it was a man named Dengler and two others, hardcases who worked for Dengler. Dengler was a killer, Hinch told him.

But what did Dengler want with the guns except to sell them? Three big Gatling guns were too much firepower for anyone not an army general. The guns were only good as value.

Who would buy them? Getts thought that was a rather easy question. Only someone like himself. And how many people were there in the west like himself who could lay out that kind of money—and who could dispose of them for a profit? Maybe two or three.

There was Martin Fields in San Francisco, John Borkman in New Orleans, and maybe Paddy Capwell in Turpin. Paddy also had an office in Hanford on the railroad where he dealt in cattle.

Paddy was the closest . . . by far.

Getts decided to go to Hanford. He and Paddy would have a little talk.

Stephan Herrington was the president's right-hand man, an advisor with no particular rank—many did not know if he held any office at all. But his power was acknowledged and almost never challenged, and he came into John Fleming's office. He stood in the doorway wrinkling his nose at the cigar smoke.

"My God, John, do you ever air this place out?"

Fleming got up at once, putting down a cigar. "Hello, Steve. Come in, come in."

Herrington pulled a chair out and sat, coughing and fanning the air. Fleming stared at him, then went across and opened a window. He came back and sat behind his desk. "To what do I owe this honor . . . ?"

"Don't get testy, John. It's just that some of us don't smoke."

Fleming forced a smile. He stubbed out the cigar in the bowl, careful not to damage it.

Herrington said, "It's about those Gatlings. Are you any closer to them?"

"I think so."

"Your reports don't show it—no reflection on you, John, I assure you. But the president is very interested in them."

"I didn't realize that."

"Yes. He wants to make sure they do not fall into the wrong hands."

"The wrong hands?"

"Mexico. The situation in Mexico right now is very bad. In fact, anything could happen and the president does not want those guns turned against *us*."

"I see." Fleming leaned back, nodding. "That had crossed my mind also."

"Where are the guns now?"

Frowning, Fleming shook his head. "We cannot be positive. If we knew exactly they would be under our control. I have two of our best men on the—"

"*Our* men, John?"

Fleming shrugged slightly. "I consider them our men. They are actually contracted from the Tanner organization."

"Why can't we use government employees in these matters?"

"Because for the most part they're incompetent."

Herrington blinked. "Incompetent?"

"And inept."

Herrington sighed. He studied his fingernails for a moment. "You say you have *two* men on the case?"

"Yes."

"Wouldn't it be better to assign more men?"

Fleming fiddled with a pencil. "Hard to say. Sometimes more men simply stumble over each other's feet . . . get in each other's way."

"And you think that would be the case here?"

"Yes, I certainly do. My orders are to recover the Gatlings. If say, a dozen men were out there, trampling the tracks out, then the men who have the guns might well bury them somewhere, or at least put them where they couldn't be found, and then when we were tired of looking for them, the guns would be brought out and sold to the wrong people. We'd have gained nothing."

Herrington nodded. "That's one way of looking at it . . ."

"I said, my orders are to *recover* the guns."

"You have an excellent argument, John . . . but I have bad news for you I'm afraid."

Fleming stared at him.

"The president wants more action. He is about to order militia troops into the chase."

"Oh my God! That would be the worst thing he could do! Can't you talk him out of it?"

Herrington shook his head. "It's been discussed for hours. He will not change his mind. I came down here to warn you . . ."

"Thanks."

"But I'd just as soon you didn't mention this little talk."

Fleming nodded. "When is he going to do this—this stupid thing?"

"Very soon. Maybe today." Herrington got up. "You'll get an official notice of it later." He went to the door. "I'm sorry, John."

Fleming watched him close the door. Jesus! Of all the stupid things! The goddam politicians weren't worth the powder to blow them to hell. He got up and closed the window. Then he picked up the half smoked cigar, brushed it off, and lit it.

Hiram Bowman reached Hanford late at night when everything was closed. He went on through the town and camped outside, hobbling the horses in a patch of grass and curling up in the wagon bed.

In the morning he hooked up again and drove back into town, spent a quarter for breakfast, and looked up Paddy Capwell. Everyone knew who he was and where he could be found. But he was not in his office. A middle-aged paunchy man explained that Paddy had another office in Turpin where he spent most of his time.

"We handle cattle sales here," the man told him, "along with a few other commodities. What did you want to see Paddy about?"

"I got something to sell," Hiram said.

"What is it?"

Hiram hesitated. "Can you buy things yourself?"

"Yes, of course. I'm the manager here."

"Can you spend a lot of money?" Hiram squinted. "I mean a lot of money."

"You mean a couple of hundred dollars?"

"I mean a hell of a lot more'n that."

The manager frowned. "What'ave you got anyway?"

Hiram shook his head. "Paddy's in Turpin, huh?"

"Yes. That's a good hundred miles east." The manager was fast losing interest in him. "Why don't you go see him?"

"Yeah, maybe I should . . ." He nodded to the other and went out to the street, leaning on the wagon. Now what? Did he want to travel a hundred goddam miles to see Paddy? But what other choice did he have? He glanced along the street. None of these merchants could pony up the thousands it would take to buy the guns.

That was a long way, a hundred miles. There could be road-agents out there, or maybe a few Indians. He hadn't heard of an Indian attack for several years, but it was always possible. They loved to get a pilgrim traveling alone.

And he didn't have much money in his kick. A few dollars and some change. He smiled ruefully to himself. Here he was with almost nothing in his pockets and a wagon full of contraband that was worth a pile. A *real* pile.

He had better get if off the main street. He climbed up on the seat and clucked up the team. The Turpin road was pointed out to him and he went down it a mile or so, past the last shacks, wondering if he was doing the right thing. If

Paddy didn't want the guns, what the hell would he do with them then?

Maybe there *was* someone in Hanford willing to buy them.

He pulled off the road into a grove of trees to think about it. A hundred miles was a long way. . . .

Pearson was a quiet town; it seemed different from the river towns and the cow towns though it was in cow country. It was probably the church, Laredo thought. It was a large white structure at the end of the main street, with a spire and a bell. It seemed to dominate the town.

And the bell tolled the hours. Like it or not.

They called first at the deputy's office. Deputy Abbott was in, considerably annoyed and apprehensive because he had just lost two prisoners. Sheriff Ankers was going to have his skin, he was sure.

"Important prisoners?" Laredo asked politely.

"A man named Dengler and another named Smith . . . gave his name as Smith anyway."

"A hell of a lot of Smiths in this country," Laredo commented. "We know him as Handy or Bert. You only had two men?"

"Yes . . ."

"That's funny," Pete said. "Dengler was traveling with two."

"Only two men when we brought them in," Abbott replied. "We found them on the road, coming this way."

"Guess one checked out," Laredo said. "How did they break out?"

"I've got a young kid holding down the office when I'm not here. They grabbed him when he got too near the cell."

"What happened to their wagon?"

"That's a funny thing. It was stolen the night before."

Laredo frowned. "Stolen!"

"Somebody pulled it out of the stable back there and drove

it away." Abbott shook his head. "Never had anybody steal a wagon before. Not out of our stable!"

"Dengler and Smith didn't do it?"

"No. They were still in the cells. They busted out the next night." Abbott looked perplexed. "What about the wagon?"

"The sheriff didn't tell you?"

"No . . . I had orders to arrest the men."

"The wagon's carrying three Gatling guns and ammunition."

"Jesus!" The deputy stared at them. "But how would anybody know that?"

"Somebody looked," Pete said.

Laredo asked, "You don't know where the wagon is now?"

Deputy Abbott looked very unhappy. "I've got no idea at all. It could be anywhere."

"Where did Dengler and Smith go?"

"I don't know that either. I had men out on the roads but they didn't find anyone." Abbott sighed deeply. "This is a big country."

Chapter Sixteen

KYLE Dengler and Handy were surprised to find Brush Creek so close. It was only ten miles away from Pearson, someone told them. It was the wild part of the county.

And damn little law, a bartender said.

They sat in a saloon and drank beer and pondered their next move. "The deputy is the only law around," Handy said. "We ought to be able to git that wagon out of the stable."

"What if he's taken the guns out of it and stashed them some'ers else?"

"Why would he do that?"

Dengler shrugged. "He might."

"Well, we ain't going to find out sittin' here. What say we go back tonight?"

"Remember, he had a posse together when he pulled us in. Some of them could be sittin' in the stable."

"Posse members is volunteers," Handy said. "Are they going to sit around in a drafty stable all night—in the dark?"

"Maybe not," Dengler admitted.

" 'Course they're not."

Dengler knew they had to go back—they had a lot of time and effort invested in the Gatlings. But was it possible the deputy would let them sit in the stable unguarded? It didn't seem likely.

Unless the deputy was a hell of a lot smarter than he looked, and was using them for bait. Did the deputy figure they'd come back for them?

Even so, they had to go back.

They whiled the rest of the day away, slept outside of town for several hours, then rode back toward Pearson.

It was very late when they entered the town. They walked the horses to a spot near the office and jail and got down. It was the quietest town they had ever been in; not even a dog barked. There was no light on in the jail office. The door was closed and it seemed deserted. Probably there was no one in the cells. There hadn't been any other prisoners when they'd been in the jail.

Handy whispered that he would slip up close and have a look and Dengler nodded. Handy was a lot smaller and more agile than he was. He watched Handy move close, then lost him in the gloom.

After a bit he heard a church bell ring, tolling two o'clock in the morning. He recalled hearing it when they'd been in the cells. A goddam mournful sound. He wondered who got up at that hour to ring the damned thing.

Then Handy materialized out of the dark. He came up close and his voice held considerable annoyance. "That damn wagon ain't in the stable."

"Are you sure?"

"I climbed in a window. There's nothing in that stable but two horses. That deputy stashed it somewheres."

They sat in the little office and Pete rolled a cigarette as they talked. Laredo said, "If someone saw the guns in the wagon . . . who would it be?" He looked at Abbott. "Who has the run of this place?"

"Me and the kid, Charlie Bowman."

"Where's Bowman now?"

"At home in bed. Those two hit him pretty hard. The doc says he'll be all right in a few days but he's seeing double now."

"So it wasn't Charlie who took the wagon. . ."

"It couldn't have been—I mean Charlie is as straight as an arrow. He wouldn't steal a turnip. I'd stake my arm on it."

"Can we talk to him?"

Abbott nodded. "I'll take you over there. He lives with his uncle and aunt."

It was a small house on a street of small, mean-looking houses. The aunt, Mrs. Bowman, let them in, surprised to see a crowd. Abbott introduced them as lawmen who wanted a word with Charlie. Charlie's not in trouble, he assured her.

Charlie looked pale, with a bandage on his head, but he gave them a cheerful smile. The head was feeling better today, he said. "Is something the matter?"

"About the wagon in the stable," Laredo said. "The one that belonged to the two prisoners. What happened to it?"

Charlie started to shake his head, thought better of it and said, "I dunno. I wasn't at the jail the night it disappeared."

"I slept there that night," Abbott admitted. "Didn't hear a thing."

"Who could have taken it?" Laredo persisted. "Who was in the jail that day, when you were there alone?"

"Nobody was," Charlie said.

"No visitors at all?"

"No, nobody—wait a minute—Uncle Hiram stopped in. But he was the only one."

"Where's Hiram now?"

Charlie looked uncomfortable. "I don't know. He—he hasn't been home for a couple days."

Laredo looked at Pete. Abbott went into the next room

and they heard him talking to Mrs. Bowman. When he came back he said, "That's right. He hasn't been home . . . since the night the wagon disappeared."

Laredo asked, "Where's he likely to go?"

No one knew.

When they went out to the street, the deputy said, "They fought all the time, Hiram and his wife. Hiram was a no-good. She won't tell you that, but the rest of us figured he wasn't worth a cowchip."

"Did he have any haunts—any close friends?"

"I know he hung out at Frenchie's place now and then. That's a saloon. But I doubt if he had many friends. He was a difficult man, usually grouchy and hard to get along with."

Pete said, "Then we can suppose he did this on his own?"

"I'm sure of it."

Laredo said to the deputy, "Put yourself in Bowman's place—if you can—and tell us where you'd be likely to go."

Abbott shook his head. "I don't know where he'd go in this town—you think he'd want to sell those guns?"

"Yes. They'd be no good to him for anything else."

"Then he'd probably go to either Hanford or Bannock."

"Those are towns?"

"Yes. Hanford's east and Bannock's west. Take your pick."

Pete dug out a coin. "Flip it?"

"Might as well."

Pete said, "Hanford's heads. All right?"

"All right."

Pete flipped the coin. It came down heads.

The day was half over and it would take them a full day to get to Hanford, but they started anyway. The weather was holding; it hadn't rained in several days and it wasn't too cold. They found a campground of sorts about halfway there. An old-timer with a beat-up wagon and two mules was camping. He asked them for whiskey and when they replied that they had none, he went back to his wagon grumpily.

What would they find in Hanford—if anything? Were they on a fool's errand? Recovering the Gatlings hadn't seemed that difficult in the beginning, but it was turning into a very complicated undertaking . . . with elements of mystery that could be confounding.

They were up early and on the road an hour after sun-up. They came to Soto Springs, a tiny hamlet by a shimmering lake, very soon. No one had mentioned the place. It consisted of a store and a saloon, nothing else . . . except a row of cubicles.

It was a stage stop, the storekeeper told them. The cubicles were for passengers forced to stay overnight. "It happens now 'n then," the man said. "Stage breaks down or they's a storm. . . ."

"How often does the stage run?"

"Once a week, reg'lar. Due in two days. The northbound went through yestiddy. You fellers goin' to Hanford?"

They were, Pete said. "You see an *hombre* with a wagon go through heading for Hanford?"

The man shook his head. "Dozen riders but nobody with a wagon."

"He might have come through late at night."

The man shook his head again. "Didn't hear 'im."

When they left the lake behind, Laredo said, "That doesn't mean he didn't roll through the place when everyone was asleep."

Pete grunted an assent.

The road wound through some low hills and followed a dry wash for a few miles with blackjack oaks like sentinels against the sky.

They came into Hanford at a walk, surprised at its

111

bustle. Far off to the left a herd of cattle was raising dust. Cowhands were prodding them up ramps into railroad cars. The town was about the size of Pearson but much noisier. The main street had saloon after saloon, and as they rode in a half dozen painted girls called to them from upstairs windows.

There were dozens of wagons along the street, a few black buggies and dozens of ponies. Could they ever locate Hiram Bowman in this commotion?

The railroad depot had a large waiting room and there was a roundhouse at the edge of town. It was probably a division point. They got down in front of the telegraph office and Laredo sent a wire to John Fleming, telling him where they were, giving him a brief history of the last week.

They would have an answer in a few hours, the telegrapher said. He recommended the Satterfield Hotel which was only a block away. They got adjoining rooms and went down for something to eat.

Laredo said, "Bowman's description probably fits half the male population of the town. Where do we start?"

"He's got something to sell. We look around for a buyer."

"Good idea."

They ate beef, potatoes, and string beans in the hotel dining room and after coffee went back to the desk. Laredo asked the clerk: "If I wanted to sell something valuable, who would I go talk to?"

"Paddy Capwell," the clerk said promptly, "if he's in town."

"Where's his office?"

The man gave them directions and they walked the several blocks and climbed to the second floor to be met by a stout, paunchy man. "What can I do for you, gents?"

"Are you Paddy Capwell?"

"I'm his local manager. Paddy's in Turpin at the moment."

Laredo showed his credentials. "We're looking for a man

who might have come to see you saying he had something to sell—"

The manager smiled. "Two days ago."

"What?"

"A man was in here two days ago saying he had something valuable to sell, wouldn't tell me what."

"What did he look like?"

The manager described Bowman. "I told him to go see Paddy in Turpin. He said he would."

They thanked the man and went down to the street.

"We guessed right," Pete said. "He *was* here." He rolled a cigarette, looking at the bustle in the street. "Did he go to Turpin?"

They had lost out, Dengler thought. The Gatlings had got away from them. The Pearson deputy probably had them stashed in a barn somewhere or other waiting to turn them over to the army. He thought about moving into the jail office with drawn guns, forcing the deputy to tell them. And the more he thought about it the better it sounded.

The deputy was the only law in town. It was the quietest town Dengler had ever seen. Probably nothing had ever happened here, and no one would expect something to happen. They would react slowly.

He and Handy would force the deputy to tell them where the wagon with the crates was, put the deputy in one of his own cells, lock the jail office, and go after the wagon. It sounded very smooth. No one would know which way they took out of town.

He mentioned the plan to Handy. "We watch the jail office during the day so we know who's inside. Then about dark we go in and find out where the guns are. We put the deputy in one of the cells, lock the office behind us—we can even put a note on the door saying the deputy is away."

"Hell, that ought to work fine." Handy was enthused.

113

"If we do it just before dark we'll be on the trail—and if there's any pursuit we'll run into the prairie and lose 'em."

"Where'll we go?"

"There's a railroad at Hanford. If there is a pursuit they might figger we went that way. But we'll head south to Bucklin. What you say?"

"I say let's do it."

Chapter Seventeen

HUEY Getts in Hanford quickly found Paddy Capwell's office and went up the steps three at a time. The paunchy manager informed him that Paddy was in Turpin and Huey swore.

The manager said, "Anything I can help you with?"

Huey considered, worrying his chin. "Maybe you can. Have a couple of men come here to sell something—"

The manager smiled. "You're the third."

"What?"

"Couple days ago a man was here wanting to sell something—he wouldn't say what, to Paddy. Said it was valuable. Then yesterday two lawmen were here asking about him. Now you. What the hell is this thing about?"

Getts ignored the question. "You said *one* man came to sell something?"

"Yes. One man. Skinny feller with a beard, lantern jaw . . . didn't look prosperous."

"Then two lawmen showed up? Were they Rangers?"

"No, government men. What's this all about?"

Getts frowned. *One* man? And he didn't fit the description of Clete or any of the others. It made him uneasy inside. Something had happened. And government men had showed up here in Hanford? Things were closing in. Maybe the best thing for him to do was clear out!

He made a lame excuse to the manager and hurried down the steps to the street. Yes, he would forget the damn guns, take the next stage west. He asked directions and hurried to the stage station.

The Pearson jail was on a sidestreet, near the corner of another, and it was no problem for them to watch the door. Dengler and Handy took turns sitting in tilted-back chairs with the doorway in view. It was tiresome and boring and they alternated sitting and standing at the bar of the nearest saloon, sipping beer.

The afternoon waned. Only a few had gone into the jail office, and each one had come out again. No one was inside but the deputy when they finally crossed the street and opened the door.

Deputy Abbott was at his desk, reading a book when they entered with drawn guns. He stared at them. "What is this?"

Dengler said, "Back in the jail, friend."

Handy locked the office door and they followed Abbott into the cell room and closed that door.

Abbott said, "What d'you want? You're the ones who—"

"That's right. We busted out of here." Dengler cocked his pistol. "Where's the wagon?"

"What wagon . . . oh, the one you were driving?" Abbott shook his head. "I dunno. It was stolen from the stable the day before you busted out."

They stared at him.

Abbott shrugged. "It's the truth. A man named Hiram Bowman stole it."

Dengler recalled the fuss they'd heard—that neither Abbott nor the young kid would tell them about. He had a terrible hunch that Abbott was telling the truth.

"Where did Bowman take it?"

Abbott shook his head again. "Every lawman in the county is looking for him."

Dengler motioned. "Get in the cell."

Abbott sighed and stepped inside and Dengler locked the door. Dengler holstered the pistol. "How d'you know this Bowman stole it?"

"He's the kid's uncle—the kid who works for me. Hiram was the only one in here that day. No one else could have known about the wagon."

Dengler grunted and went into the office with Handy. Handy asked, "Is he tellin' us the truth?"

"I think so. He don't know any more than we do." He kicked the office desk in frustration. "Shit!"

There was a county map on the office wall. Handy frowned at it. "Well, he didn't go to Brush Creek or we'd have seen him, huh?" He pointed. "There's two more roads out of here, one to a place called Damon and points south, the other goes to Hanford."

"There's a railroad at Hanford. He could load them crates on a car and go anywhere with 'em."

"Then let's go to Hanford."

Dengler nodded. It was their best bet.

A troop of cavalry came into Hanford, jingling and clattering, a guidon fluttering at the head of the column, hard-bitten troopers eyeing the upstairs girls.

Laredo and Pete Torres watched them file through the town and disappear past the buildings. John Fleming had told them the army was being ordered into the chase for the Gatlings. But what the hell could the cavalry do? The politicians were making big noises, showing the voters they were on top of the problem, even though they were only confusing it. Ordering out the army might sound good to some. It was actually nonsense.

They had made inquiries along the main street, in the saloons and stores, but no one had noticed a man of Hiram Bowman's description with a wagon. There were too many wagons, many with tarpaulins.

117

Had Bowman gone to Turpin? If they went that far and found no trace of him it meant the loss of days.

It was hard to know what to do. But one thing was certain: Bowman had stolen the guns to sell them. Was Paddy Capwell the only person in Hanford who might be able to buy them?

They made more inquiries. Enos Stiver was a pawnbroker who kept a shop near Capwell's office. Stiver was an older man, slightly stooped, with a wavering gaze.

No, he had not been offered any curious deals of late. Most of his business was in small objects. He waved his hand. "Like them you see about you."

The shop was filled with articles of every sort. Laredo did not mention guns, but Stiver was very definite; he had not paid out any large sums in months.

It was discouraging. There was no other pawnbroker in town and Stiver knew of no other person, save Paddy Capwell, who might invest large amounts in merchandise or other articles.

In the nearest saloon they ordered beer and frowned over it. Was the trail cold? Was there anything they had neglected?

It was late afternoon when they walked back to the hotel, passing an undertaker's establishment on the way. A contingent of soldiers came clattering down the street with a light wagon. They stopped at the undertaker's door and got down. There was a body in the wagon, resting on a bed of straw.

Pete stepped forward, staring at it, and motioned Laredo. The body was that of a middle-aged man, unshaven, with a lantern jaw. There were multiple cuts and abrasions on the face and neck. The soldiers carried the body inside and Laredo and Pete followed. A burly corporal was in charge of the men. Laredo showed him his credentials.

"Where'd you find the body, Corporal?"

"Eight, nine miles out, off the Turpin road. He been shot."

Laredo hadn't seen the bullet wound. "How'd you happen to be there?"

"We makin' a swing thataway and found 'im as we was coming back to the Turpin road. They's a big rock there."

"What do you think happened?"

"Somebody shot 'im off a horse."

"Did you find a horse?"

The corporal shook his head. "Whoever shot 'im, took the horse."

Laredo nodded and thanked the man. The troopers clumped out to the street, mounted up and rode away, taking the light wagon with them.

The undertaker was a seedy-looking individual in black. His name, according to the sign out front, was Tinker. He went through the victim's pockets, finding nothing. "Damn troopers went through the pockets first," he growled. "Nothing on him to say his name even."

"There's something on the belt," Pete said. He unbuckled it and held it up with a smile to Laredo. The name Bowman was burned into it.

"Hiram Bowman!" Laredo said.

"It's him all right."

"Youall know this feller?" Tinker asked. "Who do I send the bill to?"

Laredo said, "He lived in Pearson. Ask the deputy there, but the county will probably foot the bill."

Pete asked, "Was he shot in the front or the back?"

Tinker turned the body over. "In the back. I'd say a rifle shot."

They thanked the man and left. In the next saloon they sat in a corner. Laredo said, "What happened to the wagon with the Gatlings?"

Pete asked, "Who shot him?"

* * *

Enos Stiver had not been honest with them. Hiram Bowman had come to him and had offered the Gatlings for a small price. "Give me five hundred and they're yours."

Stiver shook his head. "Them's stolen property. I give you two hundred. Take it or leave it."

"Three hundred." Bowman pounded the counter. "Dammit, I hauled them a hunnerd miles!"

"It don't matter none to the deal how far they come. And besides, you sellin' me stolen property. I going to have government men breathin' down my neck?"

"Nobody knows I got them."

"Where did you get 'em anyhow?"

Bowman shook his head. "That ain't part of the deal neither. Gimme three hunnerd."

"Two hundred. That's my best offer. It'll cost me five hunnerd just to sell 'em."

Hiram shook his head. "It ain't enough. You sure that's your best offer?"

"Take it or leave it."

"Then I am going to see Paddy." Bowman walked out.

When Bowman closed the front door, Stiver yelled and snapped his fingers. Lenny Drost hurried in, cocking a revolver.

Stiver motioned him to the front of the store and pointed out Hiram Bowman who was climbing up onto the wagon.

"Get your horse and follow him. I want that load he's got under the tarpaulin. Bring it back here after dark . . . hear?"

"What about him?"

"Get rid of him. He's a drifter anyways."

"Yeh." Lenny nodded. He was black-haired and angular, wearing a blue shirt and jeans. He grabbed a coat and a Winchester and ran out to the stable on the alley to throw a saddle on a roan horse.

He shoved a Colt pistol into his belt and spurred around to the street in time to follow Hiram to the Turpin road.

Lenny was a drifter himself, or had been until his cousin

Stiver had offered him a job at manual labor. He had worked for Stiver a year and in that time had done some curious tasks, closely akin to stealing. Stiver had explained that they were simply good business.

But this was the first time he had been told to shoot someone.

He had no particular qualms about it, but he wished he was a better shot. He would have to get close to the man— and he had no idea if the other had a gun.

When he left the town behind he stayed far back of the wagon. In the first several miles, his quarry looked back once or twice to see him there . . . then slapped the reins to get more speed from his team.

The man was probably going to Turpin, Lenny thought. He dropped back farther. There were some hills five or six miles farther along; that would be a good place to close with the victim.

He passed the big rock and a mile or two later realized the man was not in front of him. Hurrying back, he saw the wheel tracks turn to take the side road. Swearing, he spurred the roan until he came in sight of the wagon.

But now the victim knew he was being followed. He slapped the reins, pushing the team into a gallop, and Lenny spurred after, dragging the Winchester out of the boot.

The road followed a dry stream that gradually deepened. In another mile the dry creek was at the bottom of a long drop. In places it was straight down . . . maybe a hundred feet. The road had become a narrow cart track hugging the side of the hill.

When the road straightened, Lenny began firing. He fired and levered the rifle as fast as he could. Most of the shots went wild.

But one hit. The man rose up and toppled sideways, falling from the wagon.

The team, frightened by the shots, bolted and ran over the

edge. Lenny reined in and watched the wagon fall to smash far below. He swore and gritted his teeth. How the hell would he get down there to get whatever was in the wagon?

He was about to get down to look at the body, when he saw the troopers. They were a half mile away, rounding a bend in the road. Had they heard the shots? It was evident they hadn't seen him yet. Lenny turned and rode back the way he had come. What the hell would he tell Stiver? That the wagon was smashed a hundred or more feet down in a steep canyon?

The troopers found the body—and did not notice the smashed wagon in the gorge. Corporal Macklin had it wrapped in a blanket and they carried it back to the town in a light buckboard and delivered it to the undertaker's parlor.

Macklin reported the incident to the officer of the day, talked to Laredo and Torres, and then forgot about it.

Chapter Eighteen

MICK Birnie had been prospecting for eleven years and found barely enough to keep him and his mule. He had made a good strike years ago and for a time had lived high. The memory of those times was what nudged him on in the lean years.

This country had nothing; he was passing through looking to go up to the Black Hills where he had heard about a new strike. He had wintered in Texas, investigated a rumor that kept him busy for months and finally petered out, and now he was following a dry streambed through the hills.

When he paused to rest a moment he noticed the buzzards. Two birds were circling just ahead, dropping down. Probably a deer had been killed by a mountain lion.

But it wasn't a deer. When he got to the spot, it was a team of horses. They had been killed instantly by a fall. Mick peered up and realized there was a road up there along the side of the hill. The team must have slipped over the edge and fallen. Someone's wagon was busted to bits—but there was no body. Maybe the driver had jumped clear.

There had been six crates in the wagon which had fallen into thick brush. The brush and the soft sand had cushioned the fall and only one of the crates was slightly damaged.

Mick was startled to see it held a Gatling gun. He knew what a Gatling was.

With a rock he hammered the boards back and dragged the crates out of the wreck. They were heavy as hell; he could not pick one up, but could drag them in the sand a short distance, enough to get them free of the smashed wagon. Then he put a rope around one and let the mule drag it to an overhang where it would be dry in case of rain. It took more than an hour to get them all under cover.

They had been covered by a dark green tarpaulin which was torn here and there, but he spread it over the crates. They would be impossible to see from up above.

That done, he frowned at the wheeling buzzards. They would give it all away. What he had found was valuable, he had no doubts. What could he do about it? Well, the first thing was to get rid of the buzzards.

He got out a shovel and began to dig a hole in the sand. He was used to digging but it took hours to dig a hole big enough to bury both horses.

As he was distributing the pieces of the wagon in the brush so they could not be seen from the road, he heard voices. Ducking down, he peered up and saw two horsemen come along the road, taking their time, peering around as if looking for something.

They did not see him but passed on by and out of sight.

After dark he moved a mile or more from the spot and made camp. As he broiled meat over a tiny fire he wondered what had happened to whomever had been driving the wagon. He thought about climbing up to the road to have a look, but it was steep and probably a dangerous climb. He forgot it and curled up to sleep.

In the morning the question remained: What should he do about the crates he had found?

He had never been in this situation before but the obvious first move was to go into town. He would ask some questions and decide what to do according to the answers.

The nearest town was Hanford. He loaded his belongings on the mule and broke camp.

* * *

Laredo and Pete Torres followed the corporal's directions. They took the Turpin road till they came to the big rock he had mentioned, and turned off south. There was a well-marked road that followed the contours of the low hills, then led them along a steep gorge where they could see a dry streambed below.

They traveled five or six miles seeing nothing of the wagon.

"It could have gone over the edge along here," Laredo said, gazing down.

"No evidence of it," Pete replied. "Whoever shot Bowman took the wagon."

"Yes, must have."

"But where did he take it?" Laredo pointed. "According to the corporal he and his men were coming from south. Remember he said they were going back to the Turpin road."

"And they didn't pass anyone with a wagon."

"Exactly. So whoever killed Bowman and took the wagon went to the Turpin road . . . and then what? Back to Hanford or on to Turpin?"

"We guess a lot," Pete said. "Did the man who shot Bowman know what was in the wagon?"

"Why else would he shoot him?"

Pete rolled a cigarette. "I wish I knew." He looked at the sky. "Might rain. You want to camp out here in the sticks?"

"No. Let's go back to the hotel."

Deputy Abbott, as soon as he was let out of the cell by Charlie Bowman who was up and around, wired the town marshal in Hanford and the marshal in Bannock to be on the lookout for Dengler and Handy.

He didn't bother with Brush Creek or Soto Springs, and there was no wire to the south.

He gave them Dengler and Handy's description with the advice that both were dangerous. And both were wanted for murder. Abbott did not say he had been locked in his own jail; that was too embarrassing.

Mick Birnie and his mule trudged into Hanford long after dark. He had almost no hard money; the livery stable owner took one look at him and refused to allow him to bed down in a stall. He found a deep doorway off an alley and slept there with the mule standing over him.

In the morning he begged in the main street till a cowhand stopped him. "If you's flat-busted why don't you go see Rever'nd Yager."

"Who's that?"

"He got a mission two blocks down."

Mick smiled. "Thanks."

The Reverend Joe Yager was a slight man with bushy hair and an eternal smile. His dark suit was rusty and he looked little more than a bum himself. He had a store building with the words HANFORD MISSION lettered across the front in blue paint. Inside were tables, chairs, cots, and mats on the floor. In one corner was a makeshift kitchen. The reverend received day-old food from the several restaurants in town and served it to all comers.

He welcomed Mick and saw to it he had breakfast. "A man ought to eat a good breakfast, brother."

Mick thought so too. Even if breakfast was only soup and bread rolls.

There were a dozen men in the long room, some sleeping, a few playing cards. Men came and went all day long, the Reverend Joey told him. "Work is hard to find in a small town like this one. What do you do, brother?"

"Prospectin'," Mick said.

"Ahh. And have you been successful?"

"Not much. Not lately anyways."

The Reverend Joey patted his shoulder. "Your luck will change, brother. Your luck will change."

Mick hoped to hell it would, and soon.

After he had eaten he sat on a chair and watched a number of men playing cards—without really seeing them. How would he go about selling the Gatlings to someone? Now that he was in town the problem seemed even harder. He couldn't show them to a buyer—the guns were miles away in a gorge.

And he knew that not everyone had the kind of money to buy them. And if he talked about them to the wrong person he'd have the law tapping him on the shoulder.

It was frustrating. But deep down he knew he was going to have to confide in someone. And not the Reverend Joey. Joey was too damned honest. Honesty was fine in church but out in the street it was a handicap.

Who could he talk to? He didn't know a soul.

But he met several men that day, casual conversations, a game or two of cards. One of the men was Lenny Drost.

Lenny had come back to Hanford, but not to Enos Stiver's shop. Stiver didn't know he was in town. Stiver would never come to Reverend Joey's Mission, not in a million years. Lenny was afraid of Stiver, the man had a terrible temper—and the money to bribe the marshal. And it was no great secret that the marshal had his hand out. Lenny had not returned with the guns and Stiver would not forgive that.

So, for want of something better, Lenny turned up at the Mission. As soon as he got a few coins together he would leave town for greener pastures.

These two, Mick and Lenny Drost, had deep secrets to conceal. There was something undefinable between them, recognized at first meeting. It drew them together despite outer appearances. Mick was older and ragged; Lenny was a tough, quick with his fists or a weapon—but upon meeting both recognized something in the other of himself.

They played cards together and talked casually at first, then more guardedly. Lenny learned that Mick had come along the hillside road to the Turpin turn-off. And Mick was suddenly reluctant to discuss it. Each time Lenny referred to it, Mick changed the subject.

127

But the time came when Lenny could hold back no longer. "You found something there, didn't you?"

It was a direct question and though Mick tried to avoid it, Lenny bored in. "What was it?"

Mick said, glancing about, "It sounds like you know."

"You found the horses?"

Mick smiled. "So it was you put 'em there?"

Lenny leaned over the table. "I damn sure the law's been out there, lookin', because the army brought in a body. Why didn't they find nothing?"

"Because there wasn't nothing for 'em to find."

Lenny took a long breath. He looked at Mick with new respect. "What'd you do with the guns?"

"Put 'em in a safe place. You shot the feller who had 'em?"

Lenny shrugged. "It was him'r me."

Mick didn't believe that for a second. The other man had probably only defended himself. But he wasn't going to quarrel with reality. Lenny was here, in one piece, and he realized that he was going to have to split the take. Now that he'd admitted he had the guns, Lenny would cling to him like a leech.

Lenny confirmed his thought. "You and me're in this together now. The guns're no good to us unless we sell 'em."

"That's right. But who'll buy 'em?"

"I think we got to take 'em to Turpin. They's a man there named Paddy Capwell—"

"I know about Paddy."

"All right. Tomorra we go get the guns and take 'em to Turpin."

"We'll have to have a wagon."

Lenny glanced around casually. "We'll steal one. I ain't got any money, have you?"

"No." Mick looked worried. "That's takin' a big chance, stealing a wagon! We ain't selling nothing from jail."

"*I'll* steal the goddam wagon." Lenny grinned evilly. "I

know where there's one I can get tonight. We'll head outta here before sun-up."

"If you can get one tonight, we ought to go tonight."

Lenny nodded.

After Lenny left, saying he had a thing or two to take care of, Mick thought about it. He would have to leave the mule behind, but he was gaining a partner. There was no way he could have lifted those crates into a wagon by himself. He didn't trust Lenny out of his sight, but he thought the other would play straight at least till they got to Turpin.

He hoped he would.

Chapter Nineteen

LAREDO and Pete sat in the town marshal's office discussing Hiram Bowman. According to the undertaker's report, Bowman had been shot once in the back with a rifle. The bullet was still in the body when found.

"A Winchester .44." The marshal dropped the lead on the desk. "Somebody was chasin' him. That's what I figger."

Pete said, "Someone shot him and took the wagon."

"Yes. I've sent wires to ever'body. So far it ain't turned up, but you got to remember they's maybe five hundred wagons in this territory, alike as two peas. And we don't know what the shooter looks like."

"Or how many of them there are."

The marshal nodded. "Could be two'r three. You fellers going to Turpin?"

"That's our next move," Laredo told him. "Thanks, Marshal."

"Oh, speakin' of wagons. We had one stole last night. That don't happen very often. I don't remember the last time. Stole out of a stable too . . . with a team."

"Who lost the wagon?"

"Enos Stiver. He's got a shop down the street."

Laredo made a face. "We've met Mr. Stiver." He went to the door. "Thanks again, Marshal."

On the street he said to Pete, "Do you find that curious? About the wagon?"

"I was born curious," Pete said. "Let's go talk to Stiver again."

They found the stooped man furious. He waved his fists, scowling. "The goddam country is getting lawless! A man's belongings stolen out of his stable! It's outrageous!"

"Was the stable locked?"

Stiver glared. "Of course not. Who locks up around here? Who would expect someone to steal a wagon and a team?"

"Someone needed it."

Pete asked, "Do you suspect anyone, Mr. Stiver?"

Stiver took a long breath. "It could be Lenny. He went out on an errand for me several days ago and hasn't returned."

"Who's Lenny?"

"His name is Lenny Drost. He's a cousin, my aunt's boy."

Laredo asked, "What kind of an errand, Mr. Stiver?"

"Nothing in particular. The kind of thing he's been doing for me for a year or so. It should have taken him an hour."

"But he never came back?"

"No." Stiver let out his breath. "I have to tell you that Lenny wasn't the best kind of boy—I only hired him because of my aunt. He's been in trouble before and maybe something caught up with him." He waved his hand. "Of course that's all speculation. I don't know what happened." He shook his fist. "I do know I've lost a good wagon and a team."

"Was there anything in particular about the wagon?"

"No, it was like others . . . but it was blue."

"Blue?"

"I had it painted blue with my name on it. Advertising, you know."

They went out to look at the stable. The wagon had been

131

taken late at night, Stiver said. "All the stores in the vicinity would be dark then. They just came in, lifted the latch and hooked up the team. Nothing to it." He shrugged. "One man or a dozen."

"And the team?"

"Two grays. I had them several years. Good gentle horses." Stiver shook his head. "Goddam thieves!"

When they left Stiver, Pete asked, "Are we looking for a blue wagon?"

"I'd bet money on it. And Lenny Drost."

"Did Lenny shoot Bowman?"

Laredo shrugged. "Stiver says Lenny went on an errand that would take him an hour. If that's so he couldn't have been out there, eight miles from town—unless Stiver is lying."

Pete pulled out the makin's and began to roll a cigarette. "Why would Stiver lie to us?"

"Maybe something happened between him and Lenny he doesn't want to tell us about."

"That's possible." Pete lit the cigarette. "You figure Lenny's got the guns?"

"You have a better idea?"

"Not me." Pete took the cigarette out of his mouth and looked at it. "But I keep wondering about all the wagons. If the man who shot Bowman took his wagon, and Lenny has the guns, why does he need another wagon?"

Laredo scratched his nose. "It's getting complicated. Unless Lenny and Stiver's wagon have nothing to do with it."

Pete sighed. "I hate to give that up. But I don't like the two wagons . . ."

"And we do know for certain that Hiram Bowman was shot in the back and killed. Let's ask about Lenny. Who would know anything?"

They started with bartenders and worked their way down the street till they came to the Mission. The Reverend Yager knew Lenny. "He was here a day or two, then disappeared."

"Without saying good-bye?"

Yager smiled. "That often happens. I wasn't surprised. They come and go . . ."

Pete asked, "Do you ask them for money?"

"No. I assume that if they come to the Mission they're flat broke." The reverend smiled. "We don't get a patrician class here. These men are all down on their luck. I doubt if Lenny had two coins to rub together."

Laredo said, "He worked for Mr. Stiver. Why would he come here? I mean he must have had some money. Stiver said he was paying him."

Yager said, "Did he get fired from the job?"

"Stiver didn't say so. He told us that he'd given Lenny an errand and that Lenny hadn't come back from it."

"Perhaps they had a falling out that Mr. Stiver didn't mention."

"Yes, that's possible."

The reverend said, "I usually find that the men stay here a day or so, then move on. Lenny was no different. Perhaps Mr. Stiver fired him, he had no money so he stayed here, then moved on like the rest."

That was possible. They thanked the reverend and went back to the hotel . . . unsatisfied. If Lenny had moved on, and if he had gone into Stiver's stable, why hadn't he stolen a horse to ride instead of a wagon and a team?

Maybe it hadn't been Lenny after all.

Where was Dengler and Handy? Could Dengler have shot Hiram and taken the wagon and the guns?

But how would Dengler know Hiram had them?

"Too many questions," Laredo said. "Not enough answers."

They were eating supper in the hotel restaurant when Pete said, "I vote we go back out there where they found Bowman's body. I'd like to look around some more."

133

"All the tracks are wiped out by now."

"I know. But that was our last connection with the guns. We know Hiram had them."

"All right. Tomorrow at sun-up?"

"Good."

It rained lightly during the night but had stopped by dawn. The sky was gray and it was chilly when they rode out of town toward Turpin.

They met no one on the road and there were no recent tracks in the dirt. At the big rock they turned off to the south and rode several miles to the spot where the corporal had said the body had been found.

"He was driving the wagon south when he was hit," Laredo said. "Agreed?"

"Yes. He was hit in the back and fell from the wagon—about here." Pete got down and indicated the brush.

Laredo stepped down and walked along the edge of the steep drop. "Then what about the wagon . . . did the team stop?"

"After the shooting? I doubt it . . . if there was no one in the wagon to stop them."

Laredo continued along the edge, then halted. "Come and look at this. Some time has gone by, but does it look as if a wagon might have gone off the side here?"

Pete frowned at the marks, then peered down into the gulch. "Maybe so. Why don't we go down there and have a look?"

"Good idea."

They had to ride several miles to find a way down, then they came back to the spot.

"Wagon tracks!" Pete said, pointing to the soft sand. "Someone was here with a wagon not long ago—maybe yesterday."

"And there's a mound over there—" Laredo snapped his fingers. "Where the horses are buried!" He looked up at the edge of the road. "They had stampeded, the wagon came off the road, and pulled the horses off into space!"

"Then the man who shot Hiram came down here and buried the horses—is that a piece of a wagon there under the brush?"

"It is. And there's more. He hid it from anyone viewing from up above." Laredo scratched his nose. "If it was Lenny, how did he know about Hiram Bowman?"

"It's too early for hard questions. Look here, under this overhang. This is probably where the guns were put. Damn, they were here all the time we came out looking—"

"On the road up there. We had no reason then to come down here."

"All right. So somebody came for the guns. Probably Lenny, because he *probably* stole the wagon. Now we know what happened to Hiram's wagon."

Pete nodded. "So we're dealing in probablies—where is Lenny now? In Turpin?"

"I'd say that's as good a guess as any."

"It's a hundred miles . . ."

Laredo looked at the sky. "We've got the day ahead of us. Let's go."

The road to Turpin paralleled the gulch for a bit till it petered out to a dry wash a hundred yards wide. With Lenny driving the buckboard they turned onto it and drove back the several miles to the place where Mick had left the Gatlings two days before.

Loading them, they spread the torn tarpaulin and tied it down securely, shortly before it began to rain lightly. It was not a dark night and they were well able to navigate. By dawn they were far along the road to Turpin.

"We're free now," Lenny said with satisfaction. "They'll never figure what we done."

It was a long way to Turpin, a long dreary ride. Neither had much to say to the other. Lenny knew nothing of prospecting and cared less as Mick quickly found out. Lenny had been working for day wages, not a topic of conversation, so there were long silent periods as the two grays plodded along.

As they came into the low hills, Lenny was thinking that it was a shame to have to split the profits from the sale of the guns with Mick. Mick's worth was over. Now he was only a liability. That thinking led inevitably to the conclusion that Mick was useless to him . . . Mick would have to go. Lenny had already killed a man, so what was one more?''

For his part, Mick was very conscious of the long silences, and became aware of the sidelong looks from Lenny, though he was able to hide his feelings. Lenny had not inspired trust in him from the beginning, and now that the Gatlings were in the wagon bed behind him, he was feeling distinctly uneasy.

When they made camp that night, well off the road so their fire glow would not be seen by a casual passerby, Mick was even more conscious of Lenny's eyes. They seemed to follow his every move. What was Lenny capable of?

They broiled bits of already cooked meat and, chewing, stared at each other across the fire. When they had finished, Mick got out his pipe, packed it, and took a brand from the embers to light it. Casually, he moved back and took his blanketroll from the wagon bed. What kind of a night was it going to be—trying to stay awake lest Lenny attack him?

The blanketroll hung up on something in the wagon and he turned his head to free it. As he turned back he saw Lenny's quick movement, and the glint of steel.

He ducked down as the Colt pistol roared. A bullet hole appeared in the wood of the wagon inches from his face. Mick scuttled under the wagon, hearing Lenny curse. A second bullet followed him, and a third.

The fourth hit him in the side. He felt the searing thrust of it and fell to his knees in the brush.

He got up and staggered on, the crazy thought running through his head that Lenny was a terrible shot or he'd be dead by now. He heard Lenny come after him, but it was dark away from the fire. He crawled under the brush and lay still.

Lenny stopped to reload the revolver, snapped the loading gate shut and came on, growling to himself. He passed by with Mick hardly daring to breathe, and kicked at the brush farther along, swearing aloud.

Mick winced as two shots were fired—evidently Lenny had seen movement or thought he had. The shots were in the other direction. Then, still cursing, Lenny came back and Mick closed his eyes. Lenny went on to the wagon.

Mick heard him hitching the team, then the wagon turned, and Lenny drove back to the road.

Mick crawled out from under the brush, feeling faint. His side was wet. He stumbled back to the fire, only sullen embers now. He put wood on and it flared up. In the light he saw his blanketroll on the ground where he had dropped it. Taking off his coat, he tore his shirt to make a compress, then rolled in his blankets and closed his eyes.

Lenny had done his best to kill him—and had almost succeeded.

He slept, waking in the gray light of morning, hearing the vibrations of horse's hoofs. Opening his eyes, he saw two horsemen approaching. Thank God it wasn't Lenny.

One of the riders got down and squatted near him. "You awake?"

"I-I'm shot," Mick said, weakly. The wound hurt like blue blazes. Everything was turning hazy as if a mist had suddenly settled down.

"Who shot you?" the man asked.

"Lenny . . . he . . . got the . . . guns."

The second man slid off the horse. "Did he say guns?"

"Yeh." Dengler nodded. "Let's see if we can fix him up. This sombitch knows where the guns are." He grinned at Handy.

Chapter Twenty

As they came up to a rise of ground, Laredo held up his hand and they reined in. There was a bloom of dust a mile or so to the right; it looked like a group of riders.

Pete said, "I think it's more cavalry."

Shading his eyes with a hand, Laredo nodded. "They're keeping busy . . ."

It was a column of twenty-three troopers led by a young second lieutenant. They approached at a lope and at a signal, walked the horses and halted a few yards away. The officer gave them a brief salute. "Morning, gentlemen . . ."

Laredo handed over his credentials. "Morning, Lieutenant."

The officer read them and handed them back. "I suppose then we're on the same mission?"

"We are if you're looking for the Gatlings."

"I am. My orders are to make a swing, cut this road and circle around to Hanford. Are we on a wild goose chase?"

"They have to be somewhere," Laredo replied.

"You're going to Turpin?"

"Yes. We think they might have gone there."

The lieutenant smiled. "Well, I have to follow orders. Is Hanford a big enough town to own a bathtub?"

"Oh yes. And some Pear's soap."

"I'll look forward to that." The lieutenant gave them another salute and nudged his horse. "Good luck."

The column jingled by, sabers rattling. The men gave them curious looks, then they were past.

Pete looked after them. "Patrol duty is the worst. Eat dust all day and army rations at night. Why do they join up?"

"Philosophy is not my best subject," Laredo said. "Let's get moving. We're probably a day or two behind."

Lenny drove the two grays hard. He stopped to water and feed them and chew on dried meat, then went on, dozing on the seat. It was annoying that Mick had gotten away from him, the little bastard was quick. But now Mick was afoot in the middle of nowhere. By the time he walked back to Hanford, days would pass.

He was also annoyed with himself for not being able to handle a gun better. But he had never owned a gun, the one he had he'd stolen from Stiver. And ammunition to practice with was expensive. Of course he'd been a day laborer most of his life and his hands weren't gun-handler's hands. To be good with a gun you had to have supple hands like gamblers. Gamblers were always good with pistols.

There was no direct telegraph line from Hanford to Turpin, but they sent wires roundabout. The fact that a blue wagon had been stolen in Hanford would be known in Turpin the next day. He could not go into Turpin with the wagon. The law would have him by the seat of the pants in minutes.

He had never been to Turpin before but from a distance it looked much like any prairie town. He halted the grays on a rise and peered at it. There was a railroad siding; he could see a line of cattle cars standing idle in the sun. Off to the right was a group of tepees where smoke was rising. Apparently some Indians were camping there—maybe along a stream.

What the hell would he do with the wagon?

The only thing he could think of was to leave it somewhere

in a ravine and ride one of the horses into town. Then he could strike a bargain with Paddy Capwell and lead him out here to the Gatlings.

That would have to do . . . though he hated to leave the guns unguarded.

It took an hour to find a suitable gully. He unhooked the team, picketed one horse in a grassy plot and mounted the other without a blanket. Lots of farm people rode without saddles or blankets—for short distances.

He was a longer way from town than he'd thought; he kept looking back as he rode. It would be easy to lose the damned wagon and not be able to get back to it.

Turpin was a more spread-out town than Hanford. There was a good road that led east and another that curled off to the south. Lenny rode back to the Hanford road and entered the town from the west, passing the usual shacks and sheds, even a sod house or two. God, how he hated sod houses. He had lived in one for a few months as a boy and still remembered the bugs that dropped from the ceiling. . . .

The second person he asked directed him to Paddy Capwell's office. It was upstairs over a leather shop. And Paddy was in, a wizened little man with a face like a monkey and quick, bright eyes that looked him over, seeming to register every detail—and appraise it.

"You've got something to sell? What is it?" Paddy motioned him into a small, cluttered office and closed the door.

"Gatling guns," Lenny said, seeing the startled look on the older man's face.

"Gatlings!"

"Three of 'em with ammunition."

"Jesus! Where are they?"

Lenny inclined his head. "Out there in a wagon."

"Are you alone?"

"Yes."

"What condition are the guns in?"

"New. Still in original crates."

Paddy smiled. "Ahhhh. We're talking about stolen articles!" He frowned. "I remember something in the papers about Gatlings being stolen—" He fiddled with a pencil. "Are these the ones?"

"Yes, sir." Lenny looked at the door.

"Don't worry," Paddy said quickly. "I don't tell anybody my business." He chewed the end of the pencil. "What you want for them? What's your name, by the way?"

"Lenny Drost."

"Izzat your real name?"

Lenny nodded, thinking he should have given another.

"All right, Lenny. I'll tell you straight. I'll buy the guns— if I can find a buyer."

"Will that take long?"

Paddy smiled. "Is someone after you?"

"There might be."

"I see." Paddy chewed the pencil. "And the guns are in a wagon somewhere . . . ? That's not good, Lenny. Tell you what you do. You bring the guns in and put 'em in my storehouse. I'll give you a receipt for them and when I get a buyer we'll talk dollars."

"I can't bring them in."

"Why not?"

"What kind of law you got here?"

"A deputy sheriff."

"If he sees the wagon—" Lenny shrugged.

Paddy nodded. "All right. Bring them in at night, then get rid of the wagon. Here . . ." He made a quick drawing of streets. "Which road are you coming in on?"

"From Hanford."

"Good. You come down here to the blacksmith's shop and turn right. It's a wide alley. You go about a quarter-mile till you see a laundry. It's a small shop with a big sign. My warehouse is next door. Can you come in tonight?"

"Yes."

142

"Then I'll meet you there, say an hour after dark. Is that agreeable?"

Lenny nodded slowly. The guns would be in Paddy's warehouse and all he'd have would be a slip of paper. . . .

Paddy correctly divined his thoughts. "This is the kind of business I do all the time, Lenny. My word is good—otherwise I couldn't stay in business a week. Your guns will be safe and if I don't find a buyer you get them back. But I think I know where I can sell them."

Lenny nodded and got up. He had to trust Paddy. There was really no other choice. Paddy slapped his back as they went out and he clumped down the stairs to the gray horse. Maybe in another day or two all of it would be over. And he'd have a wad of money in his kick.

That made him smile.

The flukey weather decided to take another turn; the sun came out and it stayed bright for several days. Winter was coming, Laredo thought, but these were the kind of days that raised a man's spirits. Far off to the right were low mountains, sketched on the sky with gray chalk. The nights were crystal clear, the stars glittering in a black void.

They came into Turpin at midday feeling rusty, needing baths and a good hot meal.

And that done, they looked up Paddy Capwell.

Paddy was cordial, very businesslike and polite. He seated them in his office after looking at their papers. "What can I do for you, gentlemen?"

"We've heard you buy and sell," Laredo said.

Paddy nodded quickly, eyes sparkling. "I turn a profit when I can, yes. I deal in cattle and land and even household goods. Do you have something for me?"

"We want to know if you've been offered Gatling guns."

"To buy?" Paddy looked astonished. "I've never even seen a Gatling gun! What would I do with one?"

"Sell it to someone else," Pete replied, amused.

Paddy shook his head. "I've been in business a long time and I've never heard of such a thing. Where in the world would such guns come from?"

"A government arsenal."

"Ahhhh. You mean stolen goods!"

"Yes, certainly."

Paddy's face became stern. "I do not deal in stolen articles, gentlemen. My books are open to the government—"

Laredo nodded. "We are staying at the Drover's Hotel if you should hear of anything. We would appreciate the information." He rose.

"Of course, of course. Good day, gentlemen." He watched them down the stairs, a smile twitching at the corners of his mouth. Oh, what an actor you are, Paddy!

Laredo indicated the nearest saloon. They went in and ordered beer, seating themselves at a side table.

"Did you believe him?"

Pete grinned. "Did you? He didn't once say, 'No.' He talked all around the question."

"That's what I think too." Laredo sipped the brew. "Either that's the way he talks, or he knows something. Which is it?"

"It's more guesswork. We'll have to watch him."

Laredo raised his glass.

Mick was unconscious when Dengler and Handy put him on his horse and held him there. Hanford was closest, so they headed that way, stopping every now and then to rebandage him. He was losing blood.

And he was very pale when they reached the town and carried him into the doctor's office.

"Put him on the table there . . ." Doctor Kranz was used to such cases. He was a short, stocky man with gray hair and thick glasses. He shooed them out and took off the bandage carefully, with his wife helping.

"Gunshot," he said. "Not bad, but he's lost too much blood."

"Too much?"

"There's nothing I can do but bandage him up and hope." He cleaned the wound and put a fresh bandage on it deftly. "Let him sleep."

To the two men he said, "He's unconscious. Is he a friend of yours or did you shoot him?"

"We brought him in!" Dengler said. "Of course we didn't shoot him!"

"Who's going to pay?" the doctor's wife asked.

Dengler gave her a bill. "He's only an acquaintance but we want him to pull through. When can we talk to him?"

"Maybe tomorrow."

"We'll be back then," Dengler said and he went out with Handy following.

Mrs. Kranz said, looking after them, "Those two are no good, Harry."

"Now, now, Bess, you say that about half the men in this town."

"Well—but there's something about them . . ."

It did not disturb Paddy Capwell in the least seeing the two government men. It was obvious they were chasing shadows.

Yesterday in the saloon he had heard some talk that Grover Shultz was in town. It had meant little to him at the time, but now he should talk to Shultz. Grover was the kind of man who would buy Gatlings.

He sent a boy out to look up Shultz. "Go to all the hotels first. He'll be registered at one of them—and if not, talk to the bartenders."

The boy returned in an hour to say Shultz was staying at the Bratton House. Paddy wrote a note to him and folded it over, sealing it with a bit of wax, and had the boy deliver it to the desk clerk.

In the course of an hour or so Shultz appeared at the office. "Hullo, Paddy. What is it?"

Shultz was a big man, heavy in the shoulders with the look of a stevedore—which he once was. Paddy asked him in, closed the office door, and gave him a cigar.

"I think we might do a bit of business."

Shultz lit the cigar with a wooden match and puffed blue smoke. "What 'ave you got?"

"I know you've got certain contacts, Grover. When I heard you were in town it saved me a wire. You were my first thought."

Shultz smiled thinly. "What the hell is it, a way to overthrow the government?"

"Well, it's a way to start, yes."

"Go on . . ."

"I've got three Gatling guns to sell. New, never out of the crates."

Shultz's eyes widened. "Sonofabitch! Gatlings!" He stared at Paddy. "Where did you get—no, don't answer that. New, never out of the crates . . ."

Paddy waited.

Shultz took several breaths, his eyes seemed to focus beyond Paddy, then he said, "When can I see them?"

"Tomorrow."

"Not tonight?"

"They'll be delivered tonight."

"I see." Shultz puffed the cigar. "You're a broker."

Paddy shrugged. "I sell what comes to me."

Shultz smiled. "So do I. One more important question . . . isn't the government after them?"

"Two government men were here already. But all they have is suspicion. They don't know for sure the guns are here in Turpin. I told them I've never heard of them. You can recrate them in my warehouse and ship them anywhere from here."

Shultz nodded. That was no problem. He got up and went

146

out to the stairs. "I'll see you tomorrow, then." He went down the steps puffing smoke.

Paddy smiled broadly and rubbed his hands.

Chapter Twenty-one

DENGLER sat on the side of the bed and looked down at Mick. "How you feeling today?"

Mick focused on the big man. "Who're you?"

"I found you out there and brought you in. My name's Jack Harris."

"Oh . . ." So this was the man; the doc had already told him two men had brought him in to town. "Thanks, Mr. Harris." His voice sounded weak to him.

"You going to be all right," Dengler said. "You lost a lot of blood. Got to make it up. What happened to the guns?"

"What?"

"I said, what happened to the guns?"

Mick stared at the other and now Mr. Harris looked like a big mean-faced man and he felt a definite stab of fear. He was helpless here in bed.

Dengler said, "Don't make up a story. Just tell me where the goddam guns are."

Mick closed his eyes, sighing deeply. He suddenly wished he'd never found the damned guns. The other pushed him.

Mick said, "Lenny's got 'em."

"Who's Lenny?"

"Lenny Drost. That's all I know."

"You two were together there—you had a fire."

"Yes . . ."

"And this Lenny shot you and took the guns, is that it?"
Mick nodded.

"Where did Lenny go?"

"I dunno."

Dengler pushed him . . . hard.

Mick grunted. "I dunno—I was running away—he was shootin' at me!" He looked at the big man who was scowling at him. It was a good story and he was going to stick to it.

"You didn't hear him go away? The wagon musta made some noise."

"I was out in the brush . . . he shot me."

Dengler let his breath out. He had gotten all he was going to get out of this drifter. He could see that. Well, he had a name . . . Lenny. He got up and went out. Mick could hear him talking to the doc in the next room. He was grateful to Harris for bringing him in, even though it was only to get information out of him.

But Mr. Harris hadn't asked the right questions. Mick closed his eyes. Could he catch up with Lenny? Maybe. Maybe not.

Lenny bought some bread and cheese from the general store and made his way back to the blue wagon in the ravine. It was a nice bright day. He laid his blankets in the shade under the wagon and tried to sleep. He had a long wait.

The day passed slowly but night came inevitably. He hooked up the gray horses while there was still light and drove out of the ravine to the road. He was ravenous. The bread and cheese were long gone and his stomach was growling. Well, there would come a day when he'd never be hungry again.

He had no watch, but when he judged it was an hour after full dark, he drove into town and found the alley Paddy had mentioned. A half mile down he saw the laundry—and Paddy standing in the shadows next to it.

When he saw the wagon approaching, Paddy pushed a door open and motioned to him to drive in. It was a barn of a place with a lantern hanging from a wire. He halted the team and watched Paddy pull the door closed, sliding a bar across.

Paddy's wizened monkey face grinned at him in the gloom. "Any trouble?"

"No. Fine as silk."

"Good. Let's get those crates off."

Working together, they pulled the crates off onto a hand-cart and trundled them to a wall of shelves. When they were all in position, Paddy covered them with gray canvas and tied it securely.

Then, standing under the lantern, Paddy wrote out a receipt, handing it over. "This is between you 'n me. Nobody else, mind?"

"I get you."

"Where'll you be if I have to reach you?"

Lenny shook his head. "I got no money for a hotel . . ."

Paddy reached into his pocket and came out with several bills. "Go over to Mrs. Fox's place. It's on the next street. There's a sign out front. She'll give you a room by the week and I'll send a boy for you there."

"All right." Lenny pocketed the money.

"And get rid of this wagon tonight."

Lenny nodded. How do you get rid of a wagon? He drove out to the alley when Paddy opened the door. Heading back the way he'd come, he decided to leave it in a ravine somewhere . . . and turn the grays loose. They were branded and he didn't want to be found with stolen horses. That could lead to serious trouble.

A mile or two out of town he left the wagon in a gorge and turned the grays loose. Taking his blanketroll, he headed for town on foot—and ran into a cavalry patrol.

They stopped him and a sergeant demanded to know his business.

"I'm just goin' into town."

"Where you come from?"

Lenny pointed vaguely to the west, "I been prospectin', but my horse broke 'is leg—" He gazed around him at the troopers. "What you stoppin' me for?"

"We looking for somebody." The sergeant motioned. "All right, you go ahead."

Lenny stepped aside and the patrol went past him. Eight men who looked bored with the duty. Lenny smiled to himself and turned toward the town. As policemen, soldiers weren't much.

If they'd searched him they'd have found the receipt Paddy had given him, dated that day, with Paddy's signature. Then he'd have been arrested for sure. He'd best put the receipt in a safe place.

The evening of the day they hit town, they decided to watch Paddy Capwell, and it proved to be interesting. Pete Torres found a niche on one side of the street, near the door that led upstairs to Paddy's office, and Laredo stayed opposite.

No one used the stairs and, as it came full dark, Paddy came out to the main street. He wore a coat and hat and turned toward the center of town at once, striding like a man who has an appointment. Laredo sauntered after and Pete dropped far behind. Paddy went into the third saloon, disappearing through the swinging doors.

After several minutes Pete followed. In five minutes he was out again. "He's gone. We've lost him."

"Damn!"

"He must have gone through and out the back. He's nowhere in the saloon. D'you think he saw us?"

"He could have . . . or maybe he's just naturally devious."

Pete grunted. "Then *we'll* have to be a little more devious."

"I was hoping we'd have something to tell Fleming. Well, let's report. . . ."

They sent the wire and returned to the telegraph office the next morning to get a reply. Fleming merely acknowledged the wire and asked if they had gone to Fowler. Laredo sent another saying they had not, that the trail had led to Turpin.

Paddy Capwell lived alone in a small house on a sidestreet of small houses. His wife had died years ago and he was used to living alone. He made himself supper and sat with a cup of coffee, staring at the opposite wall of the living room. Had he told Grover Shultz too much?

When he had looked out of the window of his office at the main street and seen the same man standing there for hours, it had worried him. Was Grover going to double-cross him? If Grover found out where the warehouse was, would he raid it? He didn't know that much about Shultz . . . but he had heard Shultz was a mighty hard man.

He had gone out the back way to meet Lenny and store the crates, then gone back to the office the same way. The man was still in the street. It would have been easy to go out the back way and go home, but then would Shultz have his office broken into to see if he was there? Or was that foolish? He didn't know what Shultz might do.

But if he had put a man to watch the door it meant something, didn't it? The watcher was not easy to spot, oftentimes only a shadow, but he was there, even when it got dark.

Finally Paddy put on a coat and hat and went down to the street as he usually did every day. He never looked around to see if he were followed, but went into Hogan's Saloon and with a wave to Hogan, out the backdoor to the alley. He jogged to the next street and home. He was positive no one came out the backdoor to follow.

He might have told Grover Shultz too much. Maybe Shultz figured him for a hick operator who could easily be fleeced.

Paddy got up and paced the room for a few minutes. The idea of Shultz was bothering him—what it came down to was—he didn't trust Shultz one damn bit. Of course that was a by-product of the business he was in, mistrust. Paddy seldom trusted anyone. And something about Shultz itched at him.

He made up his mind. He got his hat and put on his coat as he left the house. A lot of people knew about his warehouse; Shultz could find out about it easily. But not many knew about the other one—no one should know about the other one but himself and Damon. Damon was his warehouse boss, a man who had proved over a period of time that he could be trusted.

Damon lived close by with his wife and was surprised to see Paddy at his door. "Get your coat," Paddy said, and the other nodded without a question.

They hitched a horse to a light buckboard and drove to the warehouse. It was dark as the inside of a cat. Damon unlocked the wide door and Paddy drove the buckboard inside. They loaded the six crates on the wagon and drove out, locking the door. With Damon watching their rear, Paddy drove a half mile, making many turns. No one followed them.

At the other small warehouse they unloaded the crates as Paddy explained about Shultz and why he was taking precautions.

Damon said, "If it comes down to it we'll swear the guns were never delivered."

"That's right," Paddy agreed.

Lenny Drost took a room as Paddy had suggested, and settled down to wait. It might be a few days. He could not stay in the room; it was so small—only a cubicle containing a cot bed and a washstand, not even a chair—that he felt closed in. He tried to sit in a veranda chair, but finally walked into town and sat in the Lone Star Saloon with a beer in front of him.

The bartender was a very friendly sort and good at telling stories—a deliberate talent; he found his customers drank more, listening to him. In a few hours he was calling Lenny by name, and Lenny was on his tenth beer. Several others were gathered around, listening to the stories, and no one noticed the big man who stood near them, smoking a cigar, his eyes on Lenny's back. How many men named Lenny could there be in a small town like Turpin? Not many, Dengler thought.

He and Handy had spent days visiting all the saloons in search of a man answering Lenny's description. And here he was, drunk!

When he left the saloon finally, Dengler and Handy closed in, one on each side, and walked him away, Lenny's feet hardly touching the ground. Lenny was startled, for a moment not realizing what was happening to him. He stuttered and tried to protest but Dengler told him harshly to shut up.

They took him around behind the row of stores and buildings on the main street, where it was dark and quiet. They slammed him up against a wall. "Where's the guns?"

Lenny's head hit hard and he collapsed in their arms.

Handy said, "I think he's out."

"Get some water."

"I saw a pump around the corner . . ."

They half carried Lenny to the pump and put his head under it. Handy pumped water, soaking him as Lenny sputtered. But even with the water treatment he was too drunk to tell them anything.

154

"We'll have to take him somewhere and let him sober up," Dengler said. "Let's put him on a horse . . . ."

They took him out of town several miles to a wooded area and tied him hand and foot. He snored as they waited for dawn.

Chapter Twenty-two

THE next day they watched Paddy Capwell's office again, but from a distance. Laredo wondered if he had been seen from a window during his long vigil. It was possible.

They had a telegram from John Fleming, in code, saying he was doing his best to get the troops withdrawn, asking them for more information. Pete Torres wrote out a reply saying they had a very good suspect under surveillance, hoping others would contact him. They would follow up every lead. They were reasonably sure that the guns were in Turpin or the vicinity. All their indicators pointed to it.

At midday they took turns eating lunch and in a nearby restaurant Laredo picked up a local weekly that had come out that morning. In it he read that the local deputy had found an Indian with a blue wagon bearing Enos Stiver's name. The Indian stated he had come across the wagon abandoned, and the two gray horses cropping grass nearby. The Indian was not held.

When he told Pete about it, Pete asked, "Lenny Drost?"

"Doesn't it mean the guns were brought here in it?"

"That's my vote."

"He brought them here into town somewhere, then took the wagon out there and left it."

Pete rolled a cigarette and lit it. "Did Paddy Capwell buy the guns?"

"If he bought them, where would he put them?"

"Well, he buys and sells things all the time—he told us that. He must have a place to store articles."

"A storehouse," Laredo said. "Let's ask around."

They very quickly learned that Paddy had a warehouse. It was no secret. It even had his name on it. It was off an alley, next to a laundry.

When they rode around to it, the wide door was open and several men inside were talking together, apparently about some pumping machinery which was piled on the floor between them.

They walked the horses past the door and Laredo said, "Would you put the guns in there, with the door open?"

"If no one knew they were there."

"But anyone could walk in. It looks like they buy and sell right there."

Pete glanced back at the open door. "Are you saying you think there's another place?"

"I dunno what I'm saying. I'm just talking."

"If the crates were covered up who would know what's under the tarpaulin?"

Laredo sighed. "Yes, that's right. What would it take to get the sheriff to inventory the warehouse?"

"A hell of a lot of suspicion and probably some evidence. We've got one and not the other."

"You are waving the Bill of Rights at me."

Pete grinned. "I'm a college graduate. I know about such things. And probably Paddy Capwell does too."

Laredo sighed again. "Yes, I'm sure he does."

Lenny felt miserable when he woke at first light. He had vague memories of being pummeled by someone, and when he opened his eyes to see the big, rough-looking man and his lanky, grinning companion, he felt fear.

The big man said, "Where are the guns?"

Lenny blinked. There was no preliminary talk. Only a demand. He shook his head. "What guns?"

Dengler leaned forward and slapped him across the face. Lenny dropped back, feeling the hard sting of it, tasting blood.

"Where are the goddam guns?"

He took a long breath, looking at the big man's twisted mouth. There was no mercy there. He took too long. Dengler slapped him again.

"Where are the guns?"

Lenny lay full-length on the ground. His mouth was cut, he felt like he might vomit. . . .

Dengler stood up. He kicked Lenny's side. "The guns, dammit!"

Dengler drew back his foot and Lenny tried to roll away from the kick and failed. As the heavy boot struck his side, Lenny felt something crack and the pain made him cry out.

Dengler snarled at him, "Where are the goddam guns?"

Lenny gasped, "In the warehouse . . ."

"Whose warehouse?"

"Capwell's . . ." Lenny curled into a fetal position, sweat bathing his face. The pain was stabbing into him, seeming to get worse with each passing moment.

Dengler smiled triumphantly at Handy. "Capwell's."

Handy indicated the moaning man on the ground. "What about him?"

Dengler said, "Take a look around. See if we're alone."

Handy stepped up and settled himself in the saddle. "We ain't got a shovel . . ."

"All right. Take a look around."

Handy turned the horse. He made a circle several hundred yards out, seeing no one. They were well off any traveled path.

He headed back and waved to Dengler.

In a moment he heard the shot.

* * *

In town, it took only an hour to learn that Paddy Capwell had a warehouse off an alley. Dengler and Handy went to look at it late in the afternoon. It had a heavy door and from what they could see, a few high-up windows along the side. It was a barn of a place, large enough to drive several wagons into.

"It's a big place," Handy commented when they moved past. "Might take a while to find out where they put the guns."

"We'll find them. What we need now is a wagon and a good pry bar."

"What're we going to do with them guns when we get 'em?"

"Stash 'em somewhere for the time being. Capwell is going to raise hell when he finds out they're gone."

"He can't go to the law."

"No, but he'll hire men to snoop around. We ought to rent us a place to live before we bust into the warehouse." Dengler snapped his fingers. "Then we'll sit on the guns for a while and let everything cool down."

"Could we ship 'em out on the train?"

"Maybe later. We'll put 'em in different crates and do it nice and easy. Let's go find us a house."

Grover Shultz came to see Paddy again. "You got the guns now?"

"Sit down and have a cigar," Paddy said. "Let's talk about it."

"What's to talk about? I pay you, you give me the guns, and that's all there is to it."

"Let's talk about pay then. I want it all in cash."

Shultz frowned. "That ain't the way I do it. I'll give you—"

"Cash," Paddy said, making his voice very definite. "All cash on the barrelhead. No notes, no IOUs, nothing."

"Goddammit!" Shultz roared. "I been doing business up and down the river for twenny years and—"

"This ain't the river for crissakes."

"It's the same damn thing! It's just business." Shultz got up, towering over Paddy. He shook his fist. "I got a buyer for them guns. You going to make a liar out of me?"

Paddy scowled at the big man. "It ain't my fault what you told somebody. The guns is mine and I'll make the goddam rules. I want cash or nothing."

Shultz glared at him. He seemed about to explode. His face was red and his eyes seemed to turn yellow. But he managed somehow to control himself. He breathed deeply and turned toward the door. He yanked it open, looked back at Paddy and went out, slamming the door hard.

Paddy closed his eyes and sank down in the chair, letting his breath out. He had been afraid for a moment there that the huge man was going to smash him.

Shultz was mad as hell. Was he mad enough to forgo the deal and maybe inform on Paddy? A little tiny thread of gossip would start enormous trouble. And pretty soon the law would come around to ask questions, poking and snooping. . . .

He hadn't accused Shultz of spying on him, but Paddy was positive, and he was sure now that Shultz was eager to get his hands on the Gatlings. Paddy was wise in the way of deals; it might be more than just money—it might also be politics. A man as big as Shultz was probably involved in politics. And that was another reason not to trust him too far.

Well, the guns were in a safe place. Only he and Damon knew where. He trusted Damon completely. Would Shultz try to bribe him?

What would Shultz do next? Paddy spent the day worrying that question. He went through his regular routine, but the question was always on his mind.

How could he protect himself from Shultz? Should he

move the guns to another place? Without Damon's knowledge?

Was he himself in danger? That thought didn't occur to him till near the end of the day. When he thought of it he opened a drawer and brought out a collection of pistols. He had five: two derringers, a Smith, and two Colts. The Colts were big, heavy pieces and he was a small man, with small hands. The Smith felt better as he handled it. He shoved it into his belt and put one of the derringers into his coat pocket.

He knew how to fire a gun, but very little else. He would be at a great disadvantage unless he had the pistol out in his hand when trouble came. Well, he would do what he could do.

Of course he could hire a bodyguard.

He paused to consider it. He wished he knew more about Shultz. In his opinion, Shultz was capable of anything. And wasn't that good enough? It was his life, after all . . . and his property. He put on the coat and went out and down the street to Hogan's Saloon. He ordered a beer and asked to talk to Hogan.

Hogan was a squat, tough-as-nails man with a deceptively easy manner. He was bald, with arms like oaks; he wore side whiskers that made his face seem even wider. He came down the bar and leaned over. "Hello, Paddy."

Paddy nodded. How did you start a conversation about a bodyguard? He asked about business and gradually worked his way around to what was on his mind. Hogan was patient.

"You got somebody in mind who you think will harm you, Paddy?"

"I think so. Can you suggest someone?"

"Give me a minute to think about it." He motioned a barman. "Give Mr. Capwell another beer, Jake." Hogan went into a back room.

He came out in fifteen minutes with a slim young man in a slouch hat and well-worn clothes. Hogan crooked his finger and Paddy went across the room to sit at a table with them. Hogan introduced the young man.

"This's Ralph Fargo. Fargo, this here's Mr. Paddy Capwell." They shook hands. Fargo was a smooth-faced youngster and Paddy had instant doubts.

Hogan smiled, divining his thoughts. "Fargo is real slick with a pistol, Paddy. Slicker'n most. But let me tell you this. Nobody can keep you from bein' hit by a rifle from a window or something like that. Prob'ly nobody could keep some *hombre* from shootin' you on the street from five feet away, no matter how many was surrounding you."

"So you're saying, stay off the street."

"That's good advice." Hogan clasped hands on the table. "The best thing you can do is change your habits and maybe even sleep in your office now and then. Don't do nothing somebody might expect."

Paddy smiled. "Then if I do all that, maybe I don't need Mr. Fargo."

"All right. Suppose somebody comes up the steps to your office. Where are you?"

"In the office, of course."

"With the door closed . . . you got a secretary?"

"No."

"So you don't know who's out there. When you open the door—" Hogan pointed his finger. "Bang. You're dead."

Paddy nodded. "So Fargo's my secretary?"

"That's what we'll call 'im." Hogan smiled. "Do you agree?"

Paddy nodded. It all made very good sense. Anything to protect him from Shultz made sense. He shook hands with Hogan, thanked him and went out and up the street with Ralph Fargo.

There was plenty of space for another desk outside his door. He went down to the warehouse with Ralph and found a desk and several chairs, a few pictures for the walls, and a carpet.

In two hours the space looked very nice . . . except for Ralph. The boy looked very seedy. Paddy gave him some money for a new coat and shirt and sent him across the street to the dry goods store.

While Ralph was away, Paddy wrote a letter to George Finley in Blackburn, a town on the railroad seventy miles east. George might well be interested in the Gatlings. When Ralph returned, looking elegant in his new clothes, Paddy sent him out to post the letter.

Chapter Twenty-three

THEY were making no progress. Were they wrong about the guns being in Turpin? Nothing seemed to be happening. Pete Torres watched the warehouse in the alley and Laredo watched the office.

Many people visited Paddy Capwell's office during the course of a day. Did any of them dicker with Paddy about the guns? There was no way he could know. But the more he talked with people in the town, the more he was convinced that Paddy was probably the only man in Turpin with the kind of money to buy the guns.

Pete thought so too. "He's sitting on them somewhere—maybe till they are at the bottom of the wanted list, or maybe till he finds the right buyer."

Laredo tended to agree, though he was sure that Capwell would want to turn them over as soon as possible so his money would not be tied up in them.

They quickly noticed that Capwell came out of his office only now and then and always accompanied by a smooth-faced young man with quick eyes.

"He's got a bodyguard," Laredo said.

"That's a good sign . . . for us."

Laredo looked at him, and Pete went on: "He never had a bodyguard before, as far as we know. So now he's got contraband to sell and he doesn't want it stolen from him."

"It's an interesting theory. You think he's dickering with someone he's afraid of?"

"It could be. Can you think of another reason he'd hire a bodyguard?"

"He could be in some kind of business trouble that has nothing to do with the guns."

Pete grunted.

They received a wire from John Fleming saying that he was being pressured to assign more detectives to the case because it had become stalemated. The War Department wanted those guns back and the secretary had gone to the president about them. Fleming stated he could probably not hold them off much longer . . . though he realized more men would only muddy the waters.

Laredo wired back saying the troops assigned to the case had done nothing in particular and that more detectives would do the same.

The day after he sent the wire, Paddy Capwell and the young bodyguard came down the office steps to the street and went along it carrying valises.

Laredo had found a spot a half block away and was sitting on a bench in front of a photographer's shop where he had a clear view of the door which led to Capwell's office. As they passed him on the far side of the street he got up and followed, his eyes on the two valises. Was Paddy going somewhere?

He followed the two to the stage depot and watched Paddy buy tickets. When Paddy left the window, Laredo asked the clerk, "Where are those two going?"

"Blackburn," the clerk said, then frowned at him. "Who're you?"

"Thanks," Laredo said and hurried away. Pete Torres was watching the warehouse and their horses were in the livery stable two blocks farther along the street. He hurried there and yelled for the owner, Hank, saying he was going to Blackburn.

165

He saddled his horse and Pete's as Hank said, "That's seventy miles."

"South?"

"Take the road south outta town. Why you going in such a hurry?"

"Got a telegram." He swung up and rode out to the street, leading Pete's animal. He stopped at the first restaurant and ordered food to go in a sack. "I'll be back for it in fifteen minutes . . ."

He rode to the hotel and brought down their blanketrolls, telling the clerk they'd be back in a day or two. Then he went to get Pete, explaining the situation as they rode to the restaurant.

They were nearly a half hour behind the stage.

It was a nuisance, Paddy thought, having to go to Blackburn to see George Finley, but there was no other way. Finley wrote that he was a sick man at the moment. His doctor promised that he would be up and about in another few months, but for now he had to stay in bed. He was conducting business from the bed—what did Paddy have that was so interesting?

Paddy had no code with Finley and he dared not put information about the Gatlings in a letter. So he took the stage.

It was a weary, dusty journey. They stayed overnight at a way station in the middle of nowhere and arrived in Blackburn the next night, tired to death and bruised from being tossed about the last thirty miles as the stagecoach traversed some poorly maintained road.

Paddy stepped down from the coach, wincing, and waited for the boot to be opened to reclaim the valises. He did not notice the two men on the far side of the street who watched him with interest and followed him and Ralph to the hotel.

He did not notice them the next morning when they followed him to George Finley's home.

George was glad to see him. George was a big man, pale

as an enameled plate, needing a shave, but sitting up with pillows behind him. He was feeling good this morning, he said. "I feel better when that goddam doctor stays away."

Paddy closed the door and sat by the bed. "I got my hands on some contraband, George."

"What kind of contraband?"

"Gatling guns. I've got three of 'em with ammunition."

"Jesus!"

"They're in the original crates, still with the factory grease on 'em. Never been fired. You got contacts down in Mexico, haven't you?"

George nodded. He rubbed his stubbled chin slowly. "Gatlings . . ."

"Three of 'em."

"How long you gonna be in town?"

"No longer'n I have to."

George nodded. "All right. Give me time to send some wires and get replies. Where'll you be, at the Belmont?"

"Yes." Paddy rose. "What's the matter with you anyway?"

"Something intestinal the doc says. Whatever that is. He got a long name for it. Nice to see you, Paddy."

Paddy waved and went out.

A man named Lester Newby had a land office just off the main street. It was a small storefront with dozens of hand-written signs in the window. Newby handled land sales and anything else that came his way, according to a bartender Dengler talked to.

He went round to see Newby. "I want to rent a small house."

"Got three or four," Newby told him cheerfully. "You want one close in or out of town?"

"Farther out."

Newby nodded. He was a small man with thinning hair and glasses. For years he had been a drummer, selling lady's ready-to-wear. But when he married his wife insisted he stay at home, so he had gotten into the real estate business. He had a small house at the end of a street that might do Mr. Harris just fine. Mr. Harris agreed and asked to look at it.

They rode out in Newby's buggy. The house was unoccupied at the moment and needed cleaning, but Dengler was pleased with it. Newby agreed to have it swamped out the next day and Dengler put down the money.

He and Handy moved in the day after. They had no furniture and used boxes to sit on, but those things were unimportant. Handy had purchased a heavy pry bar and was positive he knew where he could put his hands on a wagon at a moment's notice.

It rained lightly that afternoon and Dengler said, "Get the wagon this evening. We'll do it tonight, late."

It was a light buckboard with a single horse. Handy had simply climbed aboard and driven it away. There had been no outcry. It was a good omen.

When they drove to the warehouse at midnight the town was asleep. It was a cold, misty night threatening rain. Dengler wrapped cloths around the pry bar, forced it between the lock and the wood of the door jamb and yanked down. The wood splintered and he pushed the door open. Handy drove the wagon inside.

Scratching a match, Dengler closed the door and found a lantern.

But they did not find the crates.

They spent an hour looking through the warehouse, pulling down boxes, prying them open. No Gatlings.

"The sonofabitch sold them," Handy said.

"Or he hid them somewhere else."

"That's his business," Handy argued. "He sold them to somebody already."

Dengler swore. That could be right. They were too late.

He knew when he was licked. They would probably never get on the trail of the guns again. It could happen with luck,

168

but it was foolish to depend on mere luck. Dengler thought about it, slept on it, and told Handy in the morning, "Pack up, we're going back."

Handy didn't argue.

Chapter Twenty-four

THE man's name was George Finley, Laredo discovered. Finley was in somewhat the same line of business as Paddy Capwell, buying and selling. Finley's office in town listed him as an agent for several eastern firms, and he operated a retail store, but everyone said, "George'll buy anything he can sell."

It was obvious, Laredo said to Pete, "Paddy came here to sell the guns to Finley."

"But he didn't bring the guns with him."

"So we'd better report it to Fleming."

Pete nodded, rolling a cigarette. "The guns are probably still in Paddy's warehouse in Turpin. We can wrap this case up. Tell Fleming to have the military raid the warehouse."

"Good idea."

They spent a half hour composing the coded message to John Fleming in Washington, and had it sent off.

That done, they headed back to Turpin.

When they arrived late the next day they found that Paddy's warehouse had been broken into by persons unknown. The warehouse manager, a man named Lyle Damon, stated for the newspaper that someone had gone through the warehouse like a tornado and it would take some time for him to estimate the damage and loss.

Laredo immediately sent off another message to Fleming informing him of the raid.

He said to Pete, "We're back where we started. Is this Dengler's work?"

"It's as good a guess as any. And if it is, where did he take them?"

"You don't suppose Paddy arranged it all—in case someone like you and me happened to think the guns were in the warehouse?"

Pete looked at him sidelong. "No, I don't think so. Why would he go to all that trouble? He'd simply move them, wouldn't he?"

"Yes, I suppose so . . ." Laredo worried his chin, frowning at the newspaper. "This man, Damon . . . it says here he's the warehouse manager. Wouldn't he know about the guns? I mean, if they had ever been in the warehouse?"

"He probably would. But would he tell us? He works for Capwell. He'll deny any knowledge. . . . "

"Maybe the guns are hidden in his house—he has to live somewhere."

Pete's brows went up. "That's an idea! Let's find out where he lives."

Paddy Capwell took the stage home with a bank draft, a partial payment from George Finley, in his pocket. He would have Damon recrate the guns and ammunition and ship them one or two at a time to Blackburn with other goods.

He and Ralph Fargo were tired and stiff when they got down in the stage yard in late evening. Paddy decided to go to the office before going home. He would put the draft in the office safe and write some notes.

At the door to the steps, he paused, telling Ralph he could go on home. "No one knows we're back. I may be an hour or two here. No sense in your staying."

"If you say so, Mr. Capwell."

Paddy nodded. "I'll see you in the morning." He went

171

up the stairs as Ralph departed. Then he halted and went back down and locked the door. He left his office door open, recalling what Hogan had said in the saloon, and laid one of the big Colt revolvers on the desk, the hammer cocked.

He did his work and no one disturbed him. He spent the night in the office, sleeping on a cot he'd had put in.

He woke in the morning as something jiggled the cot. Opening his eyes blearily, he saw them, three men in the office, seeming to fill it—and then he saw that one of them was Shultz.

Paddy sat up, clutching the blanket. "What the hell're you doing here?"

Shultz sat on the edge of the desk. "Business, Paddy. I come to see you about business."

"I got no business with you!" Paddy glowered at them, two men who looked like toughs behind the big Shultz. "How'd you get in?"

"The back way," Shultz said. "Not a very good lock on the door. You want to sit in that bed or you want to put your clothes on?"

"I want you all out of here!"

Shultz seemed very calm. "I came to get something, Paddy. One way or another."

"The guns're sold."

Shultz frowned. "You little sonofabitch!"

"They're sold, dammit, Shultz!"

"But not delivered."

"They're not mine any longer!"

Shultz turned, motioning to the two toughs. "Get him outta that bed."

Paddy fought them, but his strength was puny. They had him out on the floor in a moment, in his long-handled underwear. Shultz tossed him his pants and Paddy pulled them on, breathing hard, raging inside at the indignity. He pulled a shirt over his head and dropped into the chair behind the desk.

The cocked revolver was still where he'd put it, some loose papers covering it. Evidently Shultz hadn't noticed it. The two toughs went back to lean against the wall, staring at him with agate eyes.

As he sat in the chair, the revolver was only inches from his fingers.

Shultz said, "Put on your shoes, Paddy. We're going to get the guns."

"I told you they're sold!"

In a growling voice Shultz said, "We can do this easy or hard, whichever you want. I got the money so put your shoes on and let's go get the guns."

Paddy's heart was racing. The man would not listen to reason. But then Shultz ran rough-shod over everyone when he wanted something. He had broken into the office and now he was holding him up for something already sold! Shultz was a sonofabitch! He had brought his goons along . . . This was no more than an armed robbery! Probably Shultz would force him to tell where the guns were—then kill him.

As he looked into Shultz's little pig eyes, Paddy knew he was near death. Shultz was ruthless—he would grab the guns and never even pay for them!

Paddy reached for the cocked revolver.

He was tensed and scared to death, but the gun was his ace in the hole! He grabbed it up. The papers went flying and as his finger curled around the trigger, the pistol fired.

The lead ball smashed into the opposite wall over the heads of the two men standing there. Powder smoke spurted and Shultz yelled.

For an instant Paddy was startled by the shot. The gun had gone off before he had aimed and now he frantically clawed back the hammer.

But Shultz slipped a pistol from his belt and fired three shots at pointblank range. All three bullets went into Paddy's chest. The big Colt dropped to the floor with a thud and

Paddy slid down in the chair, one hand hanging, his mouth open in a scream that would never come out.

"Shit!" Shultz said angrily. He stared at the body, his face red. Killing Paddy was the last thing he wanted to do. But Paddy would have killed him.

Now where the hell were the guns?

The body of Paddy Capwell was not found until the next morning, by Ralph Fargo and Damon. Ralph found the street door locked which he thought peculiar since Paddy was an early riser. He went round to the warehouse, but Paddy was not there either. Damon was concerned, and had a key to the door, so he went back with Ralph.

The body was still slumped in the chair, cold as forever. Paddy's Colt revolver was on the floor, with one chamber fired.

"He shot at somebody," Ralph said. "But he missed." He pointed to the bullet hole in the opposite wall.

At Damon's suggestion, Ralph went for the law, Henry Biggs. He told Biggs of returning with Paddy from Blackburn, and parting at the street door.

"How come he hired you?" Biggs wanted to know.

"He said he'd had some threats. He kept a lot of money, too, in the safe."

The office safe hadn't been touched. It was still locked. Nothing else in the office seemed to be disturbed, as far as they could tell. Damon had been in the office only a few times, he told them; his office was in the warehouse, so there was no way he would know if anything had been taken.

"Why would somebody come up here and shoot him?" Biggs asked. He frowned at Fargo. "He never said nothing to you?"

"I told you, he said he'd had threats."

"But he never said from who?"

"No, he didn't."

"Why did you go to Blackburn?"

174

"Paddy went to see a man named George Finley."

Damon said, "Paddy did a lot of business with Finley."

"What kind of business?"

Damon shrugged. "All kinds of things, machinery, tools—ordinary things."

Biggs frowned at them. "Were they on good terms, him and Finley?"

"Very good."

Fargo said, "Finley was in bed when we got to Blackburn. He said he'd be in bed for another month or so."

"Did Paddy have any enemies you know about?"

Damon shook his head. "I don't think he had an enemy in the world."

Biggs indicated the body. "He had one."

The local weekly had a big story about the shooting. There were other shootings, but Paddy had been a well-known citizen and the circumstances of his death were mysterious. No culprit had been found; no one was even suspected. And no reason for the shooting had come to light.

Laredo and Pete Torres read the story and went to see Henry Biggs. They identified themselves and sat in the lawman's untidy office to hear about the shooting first-hand.

"There ain't a hell of a lot I can tell you," Biggs said. "We found 'im shot, three times from close range. He had fired one shot that didn't hit anybody. Nothing in the office was taken." He shrugged. "He was sure as hell murdered."

"How did the shooter get in?"

"The lock on the back door was busted into. Paddy had been sleeping in the office. There was a cot there that had been slept in. Whoever shot him got him up or Paddy was up when he got there. I think the killer got him out of bed. He didn't have no shoes on."

Pete asked, "If the killer went there with the idea of shooting Paddy, why bother to get him out of bed?"

Biggs shook his head. "You fellers got any ideas?"

Laredo asked, "Do you know about a man named Kyle Dengler?"

"Dengler . . . seems I do. He a wanted man?"

"Yes. We think he may have killed Paddy. We think Dengler and another man going by the name of Handy may be here in town."

"Why would they shoot Paddy?"

"We think Paddy had some contraband, Gatling guns. Maybe in his warehouse and—"

"That warehouse was busted into t'other day!"

"Yes. It could have been Dengler. When he didn't find what he wanted, he came to squeeze it out of Paddy."

"I'll be damned. Gatlings, huh?"

"They were stolen up in Oklahoma."

"Yeh, I remember now, readin' about it." Biggs shook his head. "Don't like these fancy killin's where you don't know who done it."

"Neither did Paddy," Pete said.

Chapter Twenty-five

LYLE Damon was very upset by the death of Paddy Capwell, and did not try to hide it. He had had a good job for years, and now Paddy's heirs might well discharge him—whoever they were. Paddy had never talked about relatives, but kinfolk always seemed to show up when there was money to be had.

His records at the warehouse were meticulous—but no records were kept concerning the small warehouse where they put items Paddy had bought in the shade. Now he alone knew about that warehouse, Damon reflected. Why should he share it with a bunch of unknown relatives? He had worked faithfully for Paddy all those years, hadn't he? He was entitled to a little something extra—like the Gatling guns.

Nobody knew about them. He had not even told his wife.

How would he go about selling them? He had never been involved in that aspect of the business and the thought of it made him very nervous and absentminded. Which he knew everyone would put down to his grief about Paddy.

Paddy had gone to see George Finley—and he was sure it was a trip concerned with the guns. He knew Finley slightly; the man had come to the warehouse with Paddy a few times.

Why couldn't he go to see Finley himself? Would that look obvious to anyone? Paddy had been extremely cautious about selling what he called dark-of-the-moon goods, and his caution had paid off. Paddy had spent no time in jail.

The warehouse was locked up now that Paddy was dead, all business had come to a halt. He was free to go. . . . He went to the stageline office; there was a stage to Blackburn the next morning, early. Damon bought a ticket. He made up a story to tell his wife why he was going, packed a small valise, and walked to the stage yard to find himself and two elderly ladies were the only passengers.

The second day, he got off the stage in Blackburn and went to George Finley's office and was directed to his home. Finley was propped up in bed and was mildly surprised to see him.

"The papers say Paddy was shot and killed!"

"That's right," Damon said. "They think someone came to rob him and Paddy fought back."

"Just after we made us a deal," Finley growled. "Paddy and I had a handshake piece of business."

"You mean the guns?"

Finley looked at the closed door and nodded. "He was going to put 'em in different crates and deliver 'em."

Damon sat in a chair near the bed. "I can still sell them to you."

"What d'you mean sell 'em! I already bought 'em! They belong t'me."

That startled Damon. "You bought them?"

"Hell yes! I give Paddy a bank draft and cash money."

Damon stared at the sick man. "There was a draft in the office safe but no money."

"That ain't my affair. I give Paddy cash money and the draft in payment in full. So maybe the man who shot Paddy took the money."

"Do you have a paper that Paddy signed?"

"Hell no. I told you it was a handshake deal. Me and Paddy never put things on paper. You know about them guns, you know they were contraband."

This was a startling turn of events . . . something he had not anticipated. He had seen the bank draft, and George Finley's name was on it, but Paddy had done much business with Finley; it could have been payment for any of a number of items. But there was definitely no money in the office.

"You box up them guns and send 'em by stagecoach," Finley said.

Damon sighed. "All right—as soon as I find them."

"What d'you mean as soon as you find them? They're in the warehouse, ain't they?"

Damon shook his head. "Paddy never kept shady goods in the warehouse. He handled that himself. I've been all through the warehouse and there's no guns there at all. I'm hoping that there'll be a note about them in the office."

Finley frowned at him. "How d'you know about them if Paddy handled them and not you?"

Damon shrugged. "Paddy told me he had them. He said he'd want them recrated one day soon." He rose to go. "I hope you feel better soon . . ."

"Those're my guns, dammit! You wouldn't be tryin' to squeeze me out, would you?" Finley waved his fist. "I don't believe a word o' that goddam story 'bout you not knowin' where they are! You know all right—or you'd never have come here. You get them guns boxed and you ship 'em here or there's going to be trouble."

Damon smiled. "There won't be any trouble. Are you going to the law about them?" He opened the door and went out quickly, pushed by Finley's wife in the hall and hurried out to the rented buggy.

But damn! He hadn't expected Finley to say the guns were paid for. Was he lying? There was probably no way to find out. Well, there was no way for Finley to find out where they were either. So it was a stalemate. But it was too bad, because it would have been a nice smooth deal to sell them to Finley.

Of course, over the years, he had built up a number of

179

contacts with other men, many of whom might be interested in the Gatlings. He would have to sit down and write some letters. The guns were in a safe place and would keep.

He returned the buggy to the livery near the stage depot and took the next stagecoach back to Turpin.

Paddy had kept a nice, neat ledger with transactions noted, dates, and costs, and in it was the address of Lyle Damon.

When Laredo and Pete went to the house to talk to him, his wife told them that since the Capwell warehouse was closed down, Damon had taken the opportunity to handle some private business which had taken him out of town. She expected him back in another day.

They thanked her and left. In the street Pete said, "What business would he have out of town?"

"It could be any of a number of things."

"Like Gatling guns?"

Laredo grinned. "If he went out on the stage, he didn't take them with him. I'll bet you a pretty penny they're still here in town somewhere."

"Then we'll keep on his tail."

They took turns watching the stage depot for the returning Lyle Damon. Pete was in the waiting room when the Blackburn stage arrived one evening and Damon stepped down and reclaimed his valise.

From the depot he walked home, only several miles. Pete saw him go into the house, then went to join Laredo. "He's here."

The next day Damon stayed in the house. On riding by, Laredo saw him once behind the house chopping wood. It was tiresome duty, keeping watch on the man.

The local weekly came out, with an item about the murder of Capwell. A relative had been notified, a cousin, apparently the only relative known, Frank Capwell. He was on his way to Turpin, and expected inside the week. The weekly speculated that Capwell would either continue the business or sell it.

Then Damon came from the house suddenly one morning and walked to the post office and mailed a half dozen letters. He stopped in a saloon on the way back and had a few beers with people he knew; Laredo watched him in conversation with several men for an hour or more. The talk did not appear to be business of any kind.

He discussed the letters with Pete. "It's very unusual for anyone to send a bunch of letters like that, isn't it?"

Pete thought so. Pete was convinced Damon had the Gatlings hidden somewhere. "Those are business letters. He's telling those people what he's got for sale."

"Won't they have to come here to see the merchandise?"

Pete grinned. "That's the minute we'll grab him—and the guns."

Laredo composed a report to John Fleming. He was sure, he wrote, that they were close to the guns. It was only a question of watching and waiting for the time to move in.

Fleming wired back that he had been able to divert a number of federal detectives to other cities, for the time being. But he would probably not be able to continue that practice long.

Upon shooting Paddy Capwell, Grover Shultz had left town in somewhat of a hurry and had gone to the home of a friend, a rancher, until the hue and cry died down.

He had read the papers eagerly and had not seen his name, so apparently he had not been linked with Paddy. Ralph Fargo, Paddy's bodyguard, had not known who he was. Neither had Lyle Damon, Paddy's warehouse manager.

But Shultz's eye fastened on that name: Damon.

The guns were not in Damon's warehouse, of that he was certain. But Damon probably knew where they were. It made sense.

He decided to call on Lyle Damon.

Damon had lived in Turpin for years so it took only a short time to discover his home address. Shultz went there alone at night, driving a rented buggy.

When Damon opened the door, Shultz saw a well-setup man of middle age, with a revolver in his belt. Shultz introduced himself as a man who had traded with Paddy Capwell and who wanted to discuss certain matters in private.

Damon asked, "Are you alone?"

"I am, sir."

Damon asked him in. It was a smallish room with heavy furniture, a fireplace, and a smell of food. Shultz sat in a stout chair and asked if they could be overheard.

Damon closed a door. "Only my wife is here." He had a very good idea why Shultz had come to call. But how did he know about the guns—unless he had talked about them with Paddy? Had Paddy been playing off this man with George Finley? It would be like Paddy. . . .

Shultz said, "I'll come right to the point, Mr. Damon. I am sure you know about the Gatlings." He looked keenly at Damon but the man's face did not change. "I am prepared to pay a fair price for them in cash."

Cash. Damon liked the sound of it. He smiled. "Let's talk about cash, Mr. Shultz."

Laredo had found a convenient vantage point to watch the front of Damon's house. There were five houses on the dusty street with vacant lots, weeds, and trees. In one of the lots were discarded wagons, broken-up crates, and other trash. He could lie there at his ease for hours, out of the sun during the day, with no possibility of being observed.

When he saw the buggy come along the street and stop in front of Damon's house, he got up and strolled that way. It was a dark night; he could see a big man get out of the buggy and go to the house but it was too dark to make out features.

As the man went inside, Laredo examined the buggy. It had been rented from Hulger's Livery in town—according to the small painted sign on the side. He scratched a match to read it.

The newcomer was in the house for nearly an hour. When he came out and drove away, the lights in the house went out. Damon had gone to bed.

In the morning Laredo confronted Jake Hulger at the livery stable, asking about the rented buggy. Hulger showed him the book.

"A man named Grover Shultz."

Inquiries brought them the information that Grover Shultz was well-known on the Big River as a dealer in cotton and corn. What he was doing in Turpin, no one could speculate unless he had come to talk with Paddy Capwell and only then learned of his death.

"Maybe Paddy wrote him about the guns," Laredo said, "so he came to buy and now he's dickering with Damon."

"It sounds good to me. But if so, why did Paddy go to see the man in Blackburn?"

"To get a better price?"

"Well, at any rate, Shultz is here," Pete said reasonably. "I think we're getting close to the guns."

Chapter Twenty-six

THE next morning, after Shultz had been to see him, Damon left the house very early, only shortly after sun-up. Pete was on watch and Laredo not due to relieve him for an hour.

Damon was riding a sorrel horse and went south along a rutted street, then turned west suddenly. Pete followed far back. When he got to the corner, Damon had disappeared. He was on the outskirts of town, only a half mile away was open prairie and Pete halted, peering round him. There were shacks along the road, a few solid buildings and nothing else. What was Damon doing here?

Walking the horse slowly, Pete examined each building closely—and saw the sorrel. The animal was tethered behind a square, peaked roof building that had the windows boarded up. Was this a secret warehouse?

Pete had a strong hunch it was. He turned the horse and went back the way he had come. Laredo was at the vacant lot when he returned and Pete quickly explained what had happened and Laredo agreed it was likely the hiding place of the Gatlings.

"If Damon is there alone, we ought to go in now."

"He'll put up a fight . . ."

Laredo mounted his horse. "It can't be helped. We'll try to take him alive."

"Should we call in the law?"

Laredo shrugged. "Do we need them?"

"If the guns are in there, we can turn over to the local law—get a receipt. That means our job is done."

"Yes, that's right. We can turn them over to Biggs, then wire Fleming and let him handle it from there."

"Agreed." Pete nodded.

They approached the peaked roof house warily. There was no other house nearby. The building had a wire fence surrounding it; the gate was ajar. They left the horses in front of the building and walked around the side under the boarded-up windows. There was a buckboard wagon behind the house and Damon's sorrel horse.

They moved to the backdoor.

Grover Shultz was a man who believed in trust—that others should trust him. He was not willing to trust them, however, any farther than he could see them.

After leaving Damon he put eyes to watch the house.

Damon seemed all right, but so had others who had double-crossed him in the past. And now that Damon had a wad of his money, Shultz trusted him even less. Damon had said the Gatlings were close by—and didn't that mean Damon could get his hands on them quickly to sell to someone else?

Shultz was prone to project his feelings onto others.

The eyes he sent to watch Damon were in a skinny little runt named Neil Yates. Long after dark, an hour after Shultz had left Damon's house, Yates prowled the street. He quickly found the vacant lot with the discarded wagon and other trash, thinking it would make an excellent vantage point.

And discovered someone was already there!

Was someone else watching Damon's house? Yates ran back to Shultz with the information. Shultz swore a blue streak . . . and ordered Yates to watch them both, Damon and whoever was in the vacant lot.

Yates watched till morning, saw Damon leave his house, and followed the big, dark man who followed Damon. When he was sure where Damon had gone, he hurried back to tell Shultz.

Laredo tried the door handle. It did not turn; the door was locked. He looked at Pete and knew the other was thinking the same thing—was anyone in the building with Damon? There was a horse outside, *and* a buckboard without a horse. But maybe the horse for it was nearby.

There could be a half dozen men inside.

Putting his ear to the door, Laredo shook his head. There was no sound from within. He drew his pistol and Pete did the same. He said, "We go in fast . . ." Pete nodded.

Laredo stepped back and kicked in the door.

One hard, heavy smash did it. The door slammed back and they jumped inside with cocked revolvers.

They were in a large, nearly empty room. On both sides were boxes and tools. In front of them was a pile of wooden furniture. To the left was a staircase.

A man's pale face came into view on the staircase and a pistol shot echoed in the room. The bullet rapped into the puncheon floor between them as Pete fired twice. They ran for the steps hearing rapid footsteps above. Laredo ran up the stairs and halted below the top. He tossed his hat up and a shot followed. Laredo thrust his arm up and fired at the sound, hearing the bullet smash wood.

Pete said, "Only one man."

"Damon!" Laredo called. "No sense getting killed . . ."

A voice answered, "Who are you?"

"Government agents."

"There's only two of you."

"But we know who you are and we've already wired the information. You're through, Damon. Come out—we don't want to kill you."

There was a long silence.

Then Damon said, "All right. I'm coming out."

"Slide your gun along the floor. No tricks."

A pistol came skittering along the hard boards. Laredo looked over the top step. Damon was standing at the far side of the room, his hands up. Laredo motioned to him as Pete picked up the gun.

Laredo asked, "Where are the Gatlings?"

"Downstairs."

They were pushed back against one wall, six crates, one slightly damaged. Laredo looked at them with satisfaction. It had been a hard trail but there they were, brought to earth at last. John Fleming would be very pleased.

Pete asked, "Who owns the buckboard outside?"

"I do—or rather, Paddy Capwell did." Damon seemed deflated. He had doubtless had ideas about selling the guns. And now he was facing a charge of possessing stolen goods.

It took half an hour to load the crates onto the buckboard, then they unsaddled the sorrel and backed the horse into the shafts and hooked up. Damon drove the wagon.

As they walked the horses around the building to the street, with Laredo in the lead, he saw the four men. They were on horseback, conferring in the middle of the road, several hundred yards away, and when they saw the wagon, one of them yanked out his rifle.

Both Laredo and Pete fired at once and the four scattered.

Laredo yelled to Damon, "Turn it, head for the prairie!" He pointed toward the west, to open space, and Damon hauled on the reins—then jumped off the wagon and ran for the building.

Laredo swore, and let him go. He swung off the horse, onto the wagon seat and Pete grabbed the horse's reins. They rumbled toward the prairie at a gallop with Pete firing over his shoulder at the pursuers.

Laredo glanced at the sky. It was after midday, but a long time until dark. He held the reins in one hand and reloaded the revolver. It was almost foolish to fire from a bouncing wagon or from horseback and expect to hit anything, but the act of firing hot lead made a difference to the man on the receiving end. He turned on the seat and fired coolly, doing his best to aim the shots. The pursuers dropped far back.

"Who the hell is it?" Pete yelled. "Doesn't look like Dengler."

"Maybe it's Shultz."

Laredo hauled in to a slow lope and began to circle toward the north. The four men dropped even farther back, and he let the horse walk.

Pete said, "They'll try to do something after dark." He peered around them. The sky was darkening toward the west. "Looks like a storm coming."

"It's beginning to smell a little like rain," Laredo agreed. "But it might hold us up."

They crossed a wide sandy wash that was running with several separate streams. Splashing across, Laredo looked back at their obvious tracks. A child could follow them and he sighed. If the storm hit them it might obliterate the tracks. . . .

Even from the highest rise they could not detect any evidence of pursuit, but of course with their tracks plain on the earth there was no need of close following. Laredo said a silent prayer for a stretch of hard or rocky ground that would not show their passage.

But his prayers were not answered till nearly dark. Then they reached a salt flat that was hard as a board and seemed to stretch for miles in each direction. They continued straight on, without variation, but as soon as it became full dark, they turned at right angles and went eastward.

Let the pursuers guess in which of three directions they might have gone.

It was a level plain and the sorrel horse pulled the loaded wagon easily. The storm they had expected came at last, first a misty, pattering rain as they struggled into oilskin slickers, then a heavier downpour that shortened the distances.

After an hour they stopped to allow the horses to breathe;

they ate some salt meat and speculated on the pursuers, then went on doggedly, and came at last to the end of the flats.

At first light they found themselves walking along the edge of a water-action cliff where there were deep overhangs. A good place to rest up, Pete said. There was a plot of grass and some sticks of trees. Laredo climbed the cliff, using a sharpened stick, and at the top gazed at their backtrail, seeing nothing that moved.

The rain had stopped long since and the air was crystal clear under heavy gray clouds. Maybe they had given the four the slip.

They took turns sleeping, two hours for each man. While Pete slept, Laredo climbed part way up the cliff again to keep watch. If they could find a cavalry patrol—. But probably Fleming had managed to get the army withdrawn, just at the wrong time to be a help to them. Their best bet now was to get back to a town and enlist the town marshal or a deputy. If they could find a town.

They found a trail, hardly a road, but it had been used a few times by wheeled vehicles. They followed it a dozen miles and at nightfall came upon a cluster of buildings which could not by any stretch of the imagination be called a town.

It had no law. The nearest law was eighty miles east, according to the barman in a deadfall, the only saloon.

Next to the saloon was a trading post, which was the reason for the several shacks being in that location. A half mile away were tepees. Roving Indians camped there, the bartender told them.

"They's tame enough some folks thinks. But I wouldn't let 'em catch me alone out on the grass."

They saw few visitors, he told Laredo. Fewer every month, it seemed like. He was going to close down and move back to civilization soon. "Let the Injuns have it all back. Soon's we go they'll burn down everything and a year after that it won't look like anything was ever here."

They camped outside of the shack cluster and the next

morning headed in the direction of the town the bartender had mentioned. Rain came down in the middle of the morning, then tapered off to a drizzle that stayed with them for hours. The wagon rattled over the sod, a lonely sound in the vastness. Pete rode ahead and out to the sides, keeping watch, but saw nothing.

But now they were leaving very good ruts behind. And no way to blot out the wheel marks.

In the late afternoon the clouds opened up and the sun came out, a welcome change from the wet. Then Pete came down from the top of a sand hill.

"Riders." He pointed to the south. "Too far t'tell how many. But there's somebody on the horizon."

Chapter Twenty-seven

Grover Shultz was disgusted. The storm had rolled in faster than he had anticipated, and they had lost the tracks. The wagon had been heading generally north, but when the rains came, they might well have turned east or west.

He decided to head straight on. It was a gamble, and if it didn't pay off he knew he was through. The salt flats went on forever and he tried to put himself in the other's boots. What would they do? They had three choices. Shultz halted and stared around him. The three men he'd hired stared at him, moving restlessly. He knew they were not eager for this long chase and wanted to get back to town.

To town. The nearest town was to the east. If he were in the boots of the pursued, he would head for town and enlist the law. Of course! It was the only sensible thing to do.

Shultz said, "We go east from here."

"It could be anybody out there," Laredo said. "Even Indians."

"It could be."

"But you don't think so."

Pete shook his head. "We've got to figure it's those four."

Laredo slapped the reins. Of course they did. But he knew they could not outrun the four. If Pete had been seen, the pursuers would make for them instantly.

He said, "Look for a place to hole up. It's no good having a running fight. We'll hold 'em off—and we've got one ace in the hole that maybe they don't figure."

"What's that?"

Laredo grinned. "The Gatlings. We'll load one and give 'em a surprise."

Pete laughed. "I never thought of that!" He galloped ahead and was gone an hour. When he returned he was far off to the left, waving his hat. Laredo turned that way, bumped across a rocky plain and came to a wide stream with Pete riding ahead. Pete halted and when the wagon came up, said: "There's a good ambush spot across the stream. It's not much more than hub deep."

Laredo followed him across, splashing in the muddy water. In another few days, if the rains kept up, the stream would rise too much to cross easily.

Pete was right. The ground sloped up from the streambank providing a very good parapet a dozen yards back from the stream. Laredo pulled the wagon in behind the rise and they hobbled the horses. It was an excellent spot. No one could get above them and they were slightly higher than the surrounding prairie. If the four men were able to track them to the stream and came across it here, they'd be at a terrible disadvantage.

Maybe a fatal disadvantage, looking into the muzzles of the Gatlings.

With knives they pried one of the crates open. The six-barrel gun was encased in grease which took an hour to wipe off. They set up the heavy tripod and affixed the gun.

"It's a mean-looking thing," Pete said. "The place to be is behind it." He loaded the upright magazine and slid it into position. "Shall we try a few rounds?"

"We might give away our surprise. The thing'll work, won't it?"

Pete checked it over. "It'll work. Now all we need is a

target.'' He fiddled with the sights. "I'll set it for two hundred yards. How's that?''

"Good.'' Laredo studied the stream. The far side was about two hundred yards distant.

They were ready.

But no one appeared. The distant riders on the horizon had not materialized. A misty rain came again, hanging like fog out on the prairie; hours passed.

"Maybe it wasn't them,'' Pete said at last. He squinted at the sky. "It'll be dark in half an hour.''

"Makes me edgy,'' Laredo said. "You ever get hunches?''

"Once in a while.''

"I think we're being watched.'' Laredo peered around, turning his head this way and that. "Can't shake the feeling.''

"They'd have to leave the horses and crawl up on their stomachs.''

"Well, they wouldn't have to come too close if they had binoculars.''

Pete grunted and took out the makin's to roll a cigarette. "How far does your hunch go?''

"What?''

"I mean are they just watching us or will they attack us?''

"They're watching us to decide on the best time to attack us. Don't you figure?''

Pete scratched a match, ducking down to light the cigarette. "I still think they'll come at night.''

"Well, we can move soon's it gets dark. If they think we're in this spot, that will confuse 'em a little.''

"Good idea. Let's put the Gatling on the wagon. It'll fire over the tailgate. . . .''

They lifted the heavy gun up and wedged crates around it. Laredo backed the sorrel into the shafts and when it was full dark they walked and led the animals toward the north. They halted a long stone's throw away and waited.

It was a long wait. The mist swirled about them, lifting

and falling, like clammy hands in the night. Then suddenly there were yells and revolver shots, a fusillade, all directed toward the spot they had occupied earlier.

The noise halted abruptly. Pete said, "They discovered no one's there." He chuckled. "They must be madder'n hell."

"Well, now we know they're still on our trail. Let's make some tracks." Laredo climbed on the wagon and gathered up the reins.

By morning they were far to the north. The river had swung away from them in the night and was now far to the west. But their pursuers were in sight and coming fast.

As they approached, they spread out and as they came within rifle range, several began firing. One of the shots hit the tailgate of the wagon and Laredo climbed into the wagon bed and settled himself behind the Gatling.

He aimed at the nearest man and turned the crank. The gun spat bullets and Pete yelled as the horse went down in a flurry of hoofs—then lay still. The three others dashed out of range.

"That'll make 'em get religion!" Pete yelled.

Laredo climbed back to the wagon seat and slapped the reins. The three men had gathered about the fallen horse. It was impossible to tell if the man had been hit also.

They saw no more of the pursuers for several hours. Then Laredo spotted them on a rise of ground in their front. They had circled around. He pointed them out to Pete and turned, moving toward the east. Whoever was chasing them was tenacious.

The rain had stopped and the clouds were boiling, moving eastward with occasional distant lightning that flickered like a snake's tongue. A wind came up, icy fingers reaching into their clothes, biting at uncovered cheeks and hands. In the last light of the fading day, Laredo counted three horsemen in single file riding along a ridge to the north. Apparently the Gatling had accounted for one horse and rider.

They halted before dark, selecting a wide, flat area with themselves in its center. It would be difficult for anyone to get close to them. Laredo's main worry was the horses; if they were killed there was no way they could move the guns. He hoped the pursuers hadn't thought of that. But they probably had.

Not long after dark the three men came at them from different directions. Bullets rapped into the side of the wagon and Laredo opened up with the Gatling, aiming at flashes. The gun roared in the night and the firing stopped.

The silence afterward was eerie.

It continued until dawn, but with first light the sniping began. Rifle shots from long range began to slice through the cold air. Pete fired back with a rifle and Laredo tried a few bursts with the Gatling, but that did not stop the snipers.

While Pete answered the fire, Laredo hooked up the sorrel and they galloped off to the southeast, away from the shots.

In several hours they came into a region of low sandhills that were partially covered with clumps of grass and low brush. Laredo kept to the low ground with the wagon and soon the sniping began again from the ridges to their left.

Halting, Laredo fired the Gatling, sweeping the ridges. The firing stopped and they went on. Then the sniping began again—and the lead horse was hit. It went down abruptly, threshed a moment and was still. Laredo swore and swung the Gatling around, pounding the near ridge line . . . and was rewarded by the sight of an arm thrown up. He must have hit one of them!

Pete grabbed the bridle of the sorrel and they left the downed horse behind. Laredo fired short bursts, hoping to keep heads down.

When they came out of the low hills, the prairie rolled away before them like a sea. Far behind two horsemen followed. Only two. Pete said, "We're wearing them down."

* * *

The two men followed them all that day; one was the big man they had seen at the warehouse earlier. In late afternoon they came to a road and halted. It looked to be a well-traveled path. "Maybe a stage route," Laredo said.

"It'll lead somewhere. I vote we go north."

"Good as any." Laredo turned the wagon.

They followed the path and in the next few miles another turned into it from the west; the ruts became deeper and the trail wider. As the day waned, the roofs of a town appeared. A sign proclaimed: EAGLETON, Pop. 593.

"Civilization," Pete said.

Laredo halted the wagon. "Maybe we should crate the gun."

"Good idea." Pete got down and they took the Gatling off the tripod and replaced the parts in the box. Any lawman would look askance at such a weapon ready for action.

Eagleton had a hotel—four rooms for rent; one was occupied by a man and his wife, travelers waiting for the next stagecoach due in three days. They put the wagon in the stable, signed for two rooms and Pete went to the general store and bought a tarpaulin.

This they stretched over the crates and tied down securely. It would keep out prying eyes, but not fingers. "One of us is going to have to stand guard," Laredo said.

"Then let's not stay."

Laredo nodded. "All right. We get a bath and a hot meal and slide out after dark. *Muy bien?*"

"You bet." Pete slipped out a cartridge, concealing it in his hand. "Who stands the first guard? Lead or primer?"

"Primer."

Pete showed the cartridge, primer up. "Your choice."

"I'll take the first then. You go get a bath."

Pete nodded and ducked out of the stable.

He was gone over an hour. Laredo was lying full-length in the stable loft, looking down at the door. He got up and climbed down a ladder when Pete entered.

"Those two are in town," Pete said.

Laredo went to the wide door and looked at the sky. It was not full dark yet. "Do you think they know we're here?"

"They probably do. There're three saloons in town. One of 'em's three doors from the hotel. That's where I saw them."

Laredo pointed to the rear door. "Let's hook up and get outta here. We can be gone an hour before they find out."

"You haven't had anything to eat."

"I'll eat later."

They led the sorrel out of the stall and hooked up. Pete went to open the rear doors of the stable as Laredo climbed onto the wagon seat.

As the doors opened, there was a fusillade of shots.

Laredo dived off the wagon and Pete spun around, flopping to the floor. The sorrel horse screamed and fell, kicking and threshing. A lantern smashed, spraying glass and one of the front stable windows dissolved in glass shards.

For a second there was silence. Laredo said, "You all right, *amigo?*"

"Yeah. I told you they were in town."

It was dark. Laredo took off his hat and tossed it aside. Outside was prairie. They had fired a second too soon, he thought. They should have allowed the wagon to get halfway through the door.

But they hadn't. From the sounds, the two had been directly in front of the door. Now they had probably moved aside. Laredo hissed at Pete. He stood in the shadow of the wall and motioned. He saw Pete move. The silence continued. Would the attackers think they had killed the two of them? They might. Laredo moved to the front end of the stable and Pete joined him.

Laredo whispered, "They'll have to come in to see if we're still alive." He saw Pete grin, a white sheen of teeth.

There had been another lantern by the front door. Laredo found it hanging from a wire. He took it down and spilled the oil on a patch of straw near the center of the stable. He showed Pete a match. "When they come in." Pete nodded.

They separated and waited.

They—whoever they were—would have to come in sooner or later if they wanted the guns. They would know the guns were on the wagon which was still sitting in the doorway with the dead horse between the shafts.

Laredo lay on the ground with the Colt revolver thrust out before him, ready to strike the match. Pete was ten or twelve feet to his right. The silence grew.

Then there was a sound.

Someone was at the wagon. Laredo blinked, seeing a vague shape climb up to the wagon bed with small scufflings. Was that another man beside the wagon?"

He scratched the match on the butt of the pistol and flipped the flame into the oiled straw. It flared up instantly, showing a man on the wagon—turning white-faced to stare in their direction. The other man fired. The bullet screamed past and Laredo's gun barked, once, twice, three times, and the big man crumpled.

He was conscious of Pete firing rapidly for a moment. The man on the wagon bed was flung back and lay motionless on the tarpaulin. The flame died and it was darker than before.

Laredo got up slowly. "Pete . . . ?"

"Never touched me."

They found a lantern and scratched another match. By its light they saw that both men had gone to meet their Maker. The big man, according to a letter in his pocket, was Grover Shultz.

John Fleming was very pleased when they telegraphed him from the next and larger town. His instructions were to send the Gatlings by the first freighting company to the nearest army post and this was done at once.

Then, Fleming said, "I will recommend that you both be given a week off."

"What a fine, generous man," Laredo said.

Pete shrugged and rolled a cigarette.

About the Author

ARTHUR MOORE is the author of twelve westerns including THE KID FROM RINCON, published by Fawcett Books. He lives in Westlake Village, California, where he is at work on a new Bluestar Western.

G. CLIFTON WISLER

************** presents **************

THE DELAMER WESTERNS